Hal looked back. He could not see his brother because of the dense cloud of flying snow dust. He called, but the screech of the wind was stronger than his shout. He would have to go back and find his brother. That should be easy — he need only follow his tracks.

But he found no tracks. They had promptly been filled by snow. Now, which nunatak had they come around last? He wasn't sure. He was getting light-headed.

'Wait a minute, Olrik. We've lost the kid.'

Olrik was only a few feet away but did not hear him. But Olrik saw him stagger. At once he reached out to help him.

'I can't see anything,' Hal said.

by the same author

**AMAZON ADVENTURE
SOUTH SEA ADVENTURE
UNDERWATER ADVENTURE
VOLCANO ADVENTURE
AFRICAN ADVENTURE
ELEPHANT ADVENTURE
SAFARI ADVENTURE**

ARCTIC ADVENTURE

by

WILLARD PRICE

Illustrated by

PAT MARRIOTT

RED FOX

A Red Fox Book

Published by Random House Children's Books
61–63 Uxbridge Road, London W5 5SA

A division of The Random House Group Limited
London Melbourne Sydney Auckland
Johannesburg and agencies throughout the world

First published by Jonathan Cape Ltd 1980

Red Fox edition 1993

13 15 17 19 20 18 16 14

Phototypeset in Baskerville by Intype, London
Printed and bound in Great Britain by
Cox & Wyman Ltd, Reading, Berkshire

THE RANDOM HOUSE GROUP Limited Reg. No. 954009

Papers used by Random House Group Limited
are natural, recyclable products made from wood grown in
sustainable forests. The manufacturing processes conform to
the environmental regulations of the country of origin.

ISBN 0 09 918321 8

To
M. V. P.
always

Contents

1	Polar Bear	9
2	This Strange Greenland	15
3	Roger and the Giants	18
4	Zeb — the Smart Guy	28
5	Who Cares about a Caribou?	31
6	Terrible Journey	36
7	Perils of the Ice Cap	49
8	Thunder River	56
9	Frozen Whiskers	60
10	Dance of the Hobgoblins	65
11	Musk-Ox in Evening Dress	67
12	Starving Is No Fun	73
13	The Man Who Ate His Foot	80
14	Ghosts Get Angry	84
15	Flight to the North Pole	91
16	The Walrus Said . . .	95
17	Roger and the Killer	102
18	His Tooth Is Nine Feet Long	109
19	Monster with Ten Arms	114
20	Living under Ice	119
21	Hal Rides an Iceberg	123
22	Hurricane	133
23	City of Polar Bears	137

24	Off to Alaska	143
25	The Well-Dressed Sea Otter	147
26	Battle of the Giants	151
27	The Whale That Sings	
	The Whale That Whistles	157
28	A Sheep Can Kill	165
29	The Moose and the Mouse	173
30	The Wild Williwaw	185
31	Orchestra of the Elks	195
32	The Horrible Grizzly	207
33	Biggest Bear on Earth	212

1
Polar Bear

Roger sat down on a snowbank. At least he *thought* it was a snowbank.

He was tired. He had been helping his big brother, Hal, build an igloo.

An igloo was a house made of blocks of snow. This one was about twelve feet in diameter and rounded off on the top. It was nine feet high. That was high enough even for Hal, who was six feet tall.

Roger shivered. 'It's as cold as Greenland,' he called.

He had often heard people say that, even in New York. Why didn't they say 'cold as Alaska' or 'cold as Siberia'? He asked Hal about it.

'Because Greenland is about the coldest spot on earth,' Hal said. 'It's the closest to the North Pole. Besides it wears a cap of ice two miles thick. That's why you're shivering right now. Because you're in Greenland.'

'Why did Dad send us here when there are so many nice warm places to go to?'

'Because a famous animal collector like Dad has to get the animals that zoos want to buy. And zoos have been asking for the wonderful animals that live

up here — the polar bear, walrus, big bearded seal, sea lion, musk-ox, narwhal, wild reindeer, caribou, humpback whale, sea otter, Greenland shark . . .'

'Hey, what's going on?' Roger yelled. 'Is it an earthquake?'

The snow beneath him was shaking violently. It had come alive. There was a deep growl. Then the head of a polar bear came up. The beast was angry because his sleep had been disturbed. With a mighty heave the great body rose, tossing Roger ten feet away head first into a drift.

He pulled himself loose and began to run. The great bear came lumbering after him. The boy staggered in the deep snow. He had once been chased by a grizzly in Canada. But this creature was big enough and strong enough to eat a grizzly.

Roger made for home as fast as his legs could carry him. Home was the igloo. Hal could have killed the animal if he had had a rifle. But he and his brother were 'bring 'em back alive' men. A dead bear would be of no use to a zoo.

Roger plunged into the igloo. The great white bear followed him. Boy and bear were alone in the snow house.

The unwelcome guest rose on his hind feet to attack this impudent human. That was the bear's mistake. Standing up he was ten feet tall. Since the roof was only nine feet high, the enormous head crashed through the roof.

What a strange sight — an igloo topped by the head of a polar bear. But Hal and Roger had built well. Not well enough to prevent the monster from going through the roof, but well enough to catch the bear between the icy blocks so he could not get down to pull that rascal, Roger, to pieces.

Hal saw his opportunity. He ran into the igloo, snatched up a piece of rope, and tied the animal's hind feet together. The rope was strong with a wire running through it. The bear roared furiously and danced a fandango to loosen the rope, but it was no use.

The front feet dangled inside and Hal promptly gave them the same treatment — or tried to. The trouble was that the forefeet were the bear's chief weapons, so strong that one swat of a powerful paw would send Hal to heaven and he wasn't ready to go there — yet. So Hal dodged the flailing feet. Luckily the big bear, with his head out in space, could not see where Hal was at any moment so his hammer blows failed to reach their mark. Hal dodged here and there — one wrong dodge and he would go to join his ancestors.

Hal finally got a loop over one of the bear's front legs. Then it was not too difficult to run the rope over the other leg and draw them together under a tight knot.

In the meantime Roger had been speeding to other igloos to get help, since two boys could not handle this thousand-pound monster alone.

An Eskimo is always willing to help, and it was only a matter of minutes before a dozen men were on hand. They weren't sure what they were supposed to do. One carried a big gun, and another came with bow and arrow. Hal, not proficient in the Eskimo language, could not tell them that the bear was not to be killed.

A handsome young man stepped forward and said, 'I speak English. What do you want?'

'We want', Hal said, 'to take this bear alive and put him in a zoo.'

'A zoo? What is a zoo?'

'A place where wild animals are cared for and everybody can watch them.'

'Yes. Very good,' said the stranger. He turned to the men with the gun and the bow and arrow. He seemed to be telling them that this was no killing job.

'What is your name?' Hal asked.

The young man was embarrassed. 'No Eskimo tells his name,' he said.

'Why not?'

'Because to an Eskimo his name is like his soul. It is a spirit. And the spirit is angry if the man it lives with tells his name. Someone else can tell you. That is all right.'

He spoke to the man next to him, who told Hal

12

the name that its owner did not dare speak. Their helper's name was Olrik.

Hal said, 'Glad to know you, Olrik.' And he clasped Olrik's hand. 'How old are you? Or is that another secret?'

'No secret. I'm twenty. And you?'

'The same,' Hal replied.

Roger had a question. 'What's the Eskimo name for polar bear?'

'Nanook.'

Hal said, 'I have a notion that all of us including the bear are going to get along well together.'

Olrik gave him a warm smile. Already they were friends.

'Now, about this bear,' said Olrik, 'have you a piece of cloth?'

Hal didn't quite see how one could tackle a polar bear with a piece of cloth. But he went into the igloo and came out with a scarf.

Olrik, hoisted to the roof by the men, tied the scarf tightly around the bear's head, completely covering his eyes.

It had a magic effect. The giant was conquered. He stopped twisting, squirming and roaring, and was as quiet as a lamb.

Then one of the cages that the boys had brought from home was placed directly in front of the entrance to the snow house.

An axe was used to break the blocks that held the bear captive. Nanook dropped to the floor of the snow house. With his legs tied and his eyes covered he could only hunch about blindly. But he presently found the outlet and stumbled into the cage. The door was promptly closed behind him.

'He's tired after all his struggles,' said Olrik. 'Polar bears sleep a lot. When he's asleep you can come in and take the cloth off his eyes and the ropes from his feet. But be very careful. If he wakes he'll be after you like a stroke of lightning. Perhaps you'd let me do it.'

'No, I'll take care of it,' Hal said.

'I will,' chimed in Roger. 'After all, he's sort of my bear. I sat on him.'

Hal laughed. 'So you think sitting on him gave you a special privilege? No, the folks back home would never forgive me if I came home alone.'

But when both bear and Hal were sound asleep, Roger slipped cautiously into the cage, removed the blindfold and untied the bear's feet. The bear woke, but there was no stroke of lightning. Polar bears are intelligent. This one was intelligent enough to know that somebody was doing him a good turn.

He rolled over and went to sleep again.

2
This Strange Greenland

'Why do they call it Greenland?' Roger wanted to know.

'Perhaps because it isn't green,' Hal answered.

'That's no answer,' Roger objected.

'Yes it is. The Danes came and made it a part of Denmark. They wanted other people to come and live here. It's the largest island in the world. Almost 1,700 miles long and 800 wide. But it's no good without people. People wouldn't come if they called it Drearyland or Deadland or No-Man's Land. So they called it Greenland.'

'But that was a lie.'

'Not exactly. It's true that most of the island is covered with ice. And what ice! Eleven thousand feet thick. If you could go down a mile into it you would find ice a thousand years old. It just never melts — except that it gets a little slushy on top in summer. It's growing thicker all the time. Come back ten thousand years from now and you'll find it a towering mountain of ice.'

'Thanks. But I don't intend to come back. I still think it should have been called No-Man's Land. Why Greenland?'

'Because', Hal replied, 'there's a broad band of green from fifty to a hundred miles wide all the way up the west coast. There are no forests. Nothing grows more than ten feet high. But there are dwarf birches, alders, mosses, saxifrages, poppies, grass, and away up here where we are, not far from the North Pole, I've heard that they can grow broccoli, turnips, lettuce, radishes and gardens of flowers.'

'I'll believe it when I see it,' grunted Roger. 'Why should these things grow on the west coast and nowhere else? It doesn't make sense.'

'They grow because a branch of the Gulf Stream flows along this coast. It brings warm water from the Gulf of Mexico. Of course, it's not so warm when it gets here. It may be about zero. But that's not so bad as on the savage east coast, where it can be terribly cold. So that's why most of the people live here, and only a few on the east coast. You might almost call that No-Man's Land.'

Roger had to admit it. Big brother had an answer to everything. If he, Roger, ever learned half as much he'd be a wise man.

'Another thing gripes me,' Roger said. 'Why is it so dark?'

'Because this is still winter. All winter there is no sun. All summer the sun shines all the time, night and day. It never goes up in the sky. It stays down near the horizon. If you didn't have a watch, you would never know whether it was noon or midnight.'

'But I have a watch.'

'Even so, it's not easy. Suppose your watch says ten o'clock. Well, which is it — ten in the morning or ten at night?'

16

Roger remarked, 'I never heard of anything so topsy-turvy. If this is winter, why isn't it pitch black? It's only a dark grey.'

'That's because the sun is just out of sight, but it's close to rising. In a few days we'll have the sun. And a couple of weeks later you'll be sick of it — shining all the time when you want to sleep.'

Roger laughed. Even this bad news couldn't get him down.

'There's one good thing,' he said. 'My polar bear. I'm going to feed him now. I don't know whether it's breakfast, lunch, or dinner — anyhow, I bet he's always hungry.'

3
Roger and the Giants

Roger got along well with animals. Perhaps it was because he liked them, or perhaps because he was not afraid of them. Maybe he was too young — fifteen — for any beast to be afraid of him.

His polar bear, Nanook, stood five feet high at the shoulder if standing on all four feet. Roger was five feet tall. So the two were a match.

A few gulps by his four-legged friend and there would be no Roger. If he had shown fear that might have been the end of him.

But he spoke gently. And he petted the monster as if he were a pussy cat. His Majesty had never been so well cared for in his life. His mother bear had not petted him, and his father had threatened to eat him. This boy fed him every two days. Previously he had often been forced to go without food for a week or two.

Nanook had never learned the Eskimo language or English. But he understood the tone of a voice. Roger's voice flowed over him softly and he replied with the best imitation of a purr that he could manage.

One day Roger told his brother, 'I'm going to let him out.'

'If you do he'll take off like a blue streak.'

Roger respected his brother's opinions. But he also respected his great bear. He very quietly opened the cage door. Nanook did not move. Roger got behind the half-ton of bear and pushed. He might as well have tried to push down a stone wall.

The bear looked back at him with big eyes that seemed to say, 'What's on your mind, kiddo?'

Roger could think of only one other way to move this mountain of flesh and bone. Perhaps it would work. Perhaps it wouldn't. He walked out of the cage door and stood twenty feet away. Then he turned and spoke. Again, the tone of his voice was easy to understand.

The great Nanook stood still for five minutes, ten, fifteen. Roger was patient. Then the King of Greenland Beasts walked out and joined his friend.

From that time on the cage door was left open. The bear went in to eat or sleep. Sleeping was good there because the floor had been covered with thick caribou hides. That was better than sleeping in the snow with rocks pushing up against your ribs.

The young Eskimo, Olrik, came to tell them that Whiskers had been seen offshore. Whiskers was the mighty bearded seal. The Eskimos called him mukluk.

Hal had heard much about the mukluk. Hal's father, John Hunt, on his animal farm near New York, had said, 'Get all the seals you can. Especially the giant bearded seal. It's twelve feet long and on average it weighs 800 pounds. An extra large one weighs twice that. Look out for the jaws. They could bite your head off. It pokes its head out of an ice hole to breathe. So do all the other seals. The difference is that you can get hold of the smaller seals and pull them out.'

'But you could never pull an 800-pound seal up through a six-inch hole,' said Roger. 'So how do you get it?'

'Go underwater. Take scuba tanks and Neoprene wet suits. The water will be cold but Neoprene will keep you warm,' said Hal.

So now, clad in the thick rubber Neoprene and carrying on their backs the tanks of air that they could breathe while searching for the monster, they joined Olrik and walked the short distance to the beach.

Roger glanced back and saw that his bear was following him.

'Stop him,' Hal said. 'Send him home.'

'Easier said than done,' objected Roger.

'You don't understand,' Hal said. 'Seals are a polar bear's favourite food. If he goes down with you and comes upon a seal, he'll start eating it.'

'I think I can teach him not to do that.'

'He'll just be a nuisance.'

'On the contrary,' said Roger, 'he may be just what we need to capture an 800-pound mukluk. He's stronger than both of us put together. But to help him learn, we'll start with something smaller.'

Olrik set off for the nearby town of Thule to hire a truck in case the hunt for the giant seal was successful. Hal also asked him to bring some men to help.

The two boys walked out on the ice and stopped at a seal hole. The seals make holes and keep them free of ice so that they can poke their heads out and breathe. The brothers stood by the hole and waited. They did not budge an inch. The slightest scrape of boot on the ice would scare away any seal.

At long last a black head came up through the hole. Hal grabbed it and tried to draw it out. Roger used his jackknife to make the hole larger.

'Great,' said Hal. 'A harp seal.' The black lines on the creature's back did look like a harp. 'This is just a pup. That's good. He's easier to handle than his six-foot father.'

Nanook, the bear, pushed forward. Was this to be his breakfast? Roger pressed his hand over the bear's jaws and he obediently backed away. Lesson one. The pup was dropped into a sack.

Later a ringed seal was caught. Again the bear was restrained. Lesson two.

After an hour they caught one more. This was a hooded seal, so called because his upper lip was so long and it flopped back over his head like a hood. Again, no lunch for Nanook. Lesson three.

All three valuable seals were in the bag.

Nanook was ready now to go down with the boys, and could be trusted not to sink his teeth into the great bearded seal if one should be found.

Roger already knew that the polar bear was a famous swimmer. It could swim six miles an hour and keep going non-stop for a hundred miles. No other bear could match this performance. Roger also

21

knew that a polar bear could kill an 800-pound bearded seal with one swat of his paw. Roger must see that this did not happen.

Olrik was back with the truck — and half a dozen men.

'We'll be ready for you if you get a mukluk. Wish I could go with you but I have no wet suit and no scuba. By the way, keep a sharp lookout for another big beast — the oogjook.'

'Never heard of it. What is an oogeljerk?'

'The name is oogjook,' said Olrik.

'Is it a seal?'

'A big one. Weighs as much as five men.'

'Well, this oogleboogle,' said Hal, 'what's its name in English?'

'Doesn't have one. But you'll know it when you see it. It twists and wriggles like a ballet dancer. It's unknown to most people here and perhaps even your father has not learned about it. But if you could get one he could probably sell it to a zoo for many thousands of dollars.'

'All right,' Hal said. 'Here goes for the mukluk and the ooglebug.'

He knew very well that the word was oogjook but he enjoyed playing with it. Olrik laughed.

Although summer was coming, plenty of ice remained on the sea. But nearby there was a narrow lane of open water, and here the two boys and the bear slipped below the surface.

The water near the surface was cloudy with plankton, tiny living cells that were the food of the baleen whale. But thirty feet down the water was as clear as glass. The temperature was close to freezing. The boys in their Neoprene suits didn't mind it.

Seal pups were much interested in the visitors, and swam all around them. They came close and nibbled Roger's hands. They cavorted and scampered like children let out of school. Hal's watertight torch lit up the lively dance of the little fellows.

But even the hungry bear paid no attention to them.

Fish in all colours swam about, and the sea floor was a fairyland with shells of all sorts, crabs with rainbow backs, and swaying sea fans rooted in the bottom and looking exactly like plants — but Hal knew they were animals. What a sight — an animal with roots in the ground.

Then a mukluk hove into sight. The bearded seal was known to be a noisy fellow. 'Chuck-chuck-chuck' was his song, but sung so loudly that he could be heard plainly through the water. He came close and squinted with weak eyes at these curious creatures who had invaded his territory.

Hal at once threw a loop of rawhide rope over the big fellow's head. He and Roger began towing the monster to the open break in the ice.

They soon found that they were as weak as cats when it came to towing an 800-pound monster.

Instead of them towing him, he was towing them. His great fins were like broad paddles, and with very little effort he could pull these two-legged beasts far away under the ice.

The bear! Nanook could help. Roger searched for him. His large pet had disappeared. Roger looked

up, and there was the bear at the surface getting a breath of air.

Of course Nanook had no scuba. He must go up to the surface for air. But why did it happen just now when he was so badly needed?

He came at last, peering about for his friends. Then he saw them far away and deep down, at the mercy of the big seal.

Nanook sank to join them, and was he welcome! Roger put the end of the line between the bear's teeth. It grew taut and the surprised mukluk paddled in vain. The boys swam toward the open water lane, and the 1,000-pound bear had no trouble in towing the bearded seal, whose whiskers trembled with astonishment as he was pulled into the water lane where the men waited at the edge of the ice.

He kept chuck-chuck-chucking as he was lifted up on to the ice and then slid up a ramp on to the truck.

'Great,' shouted Olrik. 'You did a fine job.'

'We didn't do it,' Hal said.

'Then who did?'

'Our four-footed giant. Without him the whole thing would have been a flop.'

'Well, jump on the truck and we'll go to town.'

'Not quite yet,' said Hal. 'We saw something else that may have been the oogjook you were talking about. We'll go back down and try to get it.'

So they went down, and saw to it that their bear went with them. They knew now that they could do nothing without him.

What they had seen before was still there. It did look as if it weighed as much as five men, and it squirmed, wriggled and twisted in a crazy dance.

They lassoed it and gave the end of the rope to their big pet. He dutifully hauled it, still wriggling, to the waiting men, who put it on the truck and tied it down. The bag of smaller seals was also loaded.

'Where to?' Olrik asked.

'To the Thule air base,' Hal said. 'We'll charter one of those flying box-cars, I think you call it a skyvan, and we'll send it off tonight to our animal farm near New York. I'll telegraph Dad right now to watch for it.'

He wired his father:

SENDING YOU TONIGHT BY SKYVAN HARP SEAL, RINGED SEAL, HOODED SEAL, HUGE BEARDED SEAL, AND AN OOGJOOK — DON'T LAUGH — THEY WILL ARRIVE AT YOUR PLACE TOMORROW MORNING. ALSO HAVE POLAR BEAR, BUT WILL KEEP HIM A WHILE. WE NEED HIM

LOVE, HAL

'There's one thing I don't understand,' Roger said after they had returned to their igloo. 'Won't those seals die because there's no water in that plane?'

'They'll be all right,' Hal said. 'Long, long ago seals were land animals. In a way they still are. They have no gills like a fish to get oxygen from the water. They have to come up to breathe. They took to the sea because they could find food there. But they no sooner eat than they pop out of the sea. You remember Glacier Bay, Alaska?'

'Sure.'

'What did you see there?'

'Hundreds of seals, each one sitting on a floating block of ice.'

'Exactly. They liked to spend most of their time out of the water. And you remember the great rocks offshore along the Oregon coast. What did you see there?'

Roger answered, 'We didn't actually see the rocks at all, because they were completely covered with seals.'

'Right. They like to leave the sea, except when they are hungry. So you don't need to worry about their one night in the skyvan. When they get to the farm they can use the lake if they want to because there are fish in it. But when we get home I'll bet we find them perched on the rocks, enjoying the fresh air.'

4
Zeb — the Smart Guy

The hole in the roof made by the great bear had been mended. Now Hal, Roger and Olrik sat in the warm snow house, chatting comfortably.

'By the way,' said Hal, 'where did you learn English?'

The Eskimo answered, 'In your country. I spent two years at Harvard. Later I'll go again and finish.'

Hal was astonished. 'I'll bet you're about the only Eskimo who has studied abroad.'

Olrik smiled. 'Many of our people have gone to England or America to study. Especially they want to learn English.'

'Why English?'

'So they can get a job when they come back. Did you realize that we have six thousand Americans and English in Greenland? They run most of the industries here and the two big airports — one at Thule and one at Sondre Stromfjord. If an Eskimo wants a job he'll be more likely to get it if he can speak English.'

'But Denmark owns Greenland. Aren't there a lot of Danes here?'

'Yes — and they're fine people — but they don't have the technical skill of the British and the Yanks.'

'I heard,' said a rough-looking fellow who had just come in. 'You're right. We're the smart ones. You Eskimos are the dumbest people on earth. And I mean you.'

He was looking straight at Olrik. Olrik said nothing.

Hal objected. 'Hold your horses, Zeb. They told me your name. You were here with the men who helped after the big bear bust our roof. And I recollect that you stood behind and did nothing.'

'Why should I mix with a pack of Eskimos?' blurted Zeb. 'I keep better company than those ignorant blokes.' Again he stared at Olrik.

'What was your college?' Hal asked.

'College of hard knocks.'

'Do you know,' said Hal, 'that you're insulting a Harvard man?'

'What's that?'

'A man who has studied at Harvard.'

'Don't know any jerk town named Harbard. Me — I'm from New York — biggest city in the world. And I've come here to get my pay.'

'Pay for what?'

'Helping save your silly snow house.'

'You didn't turn a finger to save anything. The Eskimos helped —just to be friendly — and they wouldn't take a cent. But I'll pay you to get rid of you.' He pulled out a five-dollar bill and slapped it into Zeb's hand.

'Five dollars,' grunted Zeb. 'It ought to be fifty.'

'I'll give you fifty — fifty punches — if you don't

get out.' Soft-spoken Hal was really losing his temper.

Zeb went out with a final threat. 'I'll see you again — you four-flusher.'

There was a shot. Hal was out at once. Nanook, who had been sleeping in the lee of the igloo, was on his feet growling. The rascal had tried to kill their pet bear. Hal and Roger felt Nanook's hide. There was only a scratch near the neck.

Zeb was gone. He was so poor a shot that even a target as huge as a 1,000-pound bear had lost only a few hairs.

5
Who Cares about a Caribou?

The boys cared when one day a caribou came sliding down the hill behind the igloo, broke the wall, and fell in.

A caribou in the house! That was just too much.

Was it bad luck or good luck? Dad had asked the boys to get a caribou. And now one had been delivered to them.

The caribou belongs to the deer family. He is sometimes called the northern deer. But he differs from the deer we are used to. He doesn't have lovely brown eyes, and he's not gentle and friendly.

This one began thrashing about wildly. For some reason, he didn't feel at home in an igloo. His magnificent antlers ploughed into the kettle, the lamps, the pans, the dishes, and sent them all flying.

'Let's get out of here, quick,' said Hal.

They got out but not before they learned that the sharp horns of the caribou don't feel too good when they penetrate tender parts of the human body.

To the caribou this was not a home but a prison which he would tear to bits. He was dangerous at

31

both ends — he had his horns in front and his heels behind.

The caribou is famous for his kick. It can kill, and has killed many interfering animals including the two-legged kind that call themselves men.

'He'll rip the igloo to pieces,' Hal said.

He was not exaggerating. The horns were tearing down the snow blocks on one side of the igloo and those terrible heels were turning the other wall into snow-dust.

The noise of clashing pots and pans brought Eskimos to see what was going on. Among them was Olrik.

'Why did you put him in the igloo?' Olrik wanted to know.

'We didn't invite him,' Hal said. 'He invited himself. What do you do in a case like this?'

'Darned if I know,' said Olrik. 'That's one thing Harvard didn't teach us.'

Zeb arrived. He knew just what to do. He sneaked in over the fallen blocks of snow and grabbed the caribou's stubby tail. At once the beast kicked Zeb in the stomach and sent him soaring ten feet away to land on a sharp rock. Zeb bent double, clutching his midriff and whimpering like a baby. He complained to Hal.

'You've got to pay me for this.'

The fellow always wanted money for doing nothing.

Hal didn't answer. He couldn't waste time on a crybaby.

The igloo was now completely ruined. The caribou plunged out straight for the boys. Hal seized the

horns and was lifted eight feet off the ground. Down
he came but he still hung on. There were plenty of
horns to go round, so Olrik and Roger took hold and
brought the animal to a standstill.

Zeb, holding his stomach with one hand and a
whip in the other, said, 'I'll teach the brute.'

As the whip came down Roger caught it and
pulled it out of Zeb's hand.

'You interfering upstart,' Zeb cried. 'What do you
know about wild beasts?'

'Not much,' Roger said. 'But I know a whip is no
good if you want to calm down a terrified animal.'

Still holding a horn with one hand he used his
other hand to stroke the neck of the excited animal
and he spoke sweet nothings into a big ear. He kept
this up for a good ten minutes, stroking, speaking
softly.

It was the old Roger magic. The animal had given up struggling. His eyes were fixed upon the boy. After all, he was just a boy and not worth killing. And he didn't mean any harm.

It was lucky for Roger that it is not difficult to tame a caribou. Thousands of them have been tamed by the Eskimos of northern Canada and Greenland. They have been harnessed and can pull a plough or a wagon as well as any horse or ox. In fact they are much better than an ox. One caribou can draw a sledge with two men on it at a speed of up to eighteen miles an hour. To become tame, all they need is a little understanding.

Roger noticed that the caribou's feet were as big as soup plates.

'That's so he can walk on snow without sinking in,' Olrik said.

'What's that funny flat bone that looks like a shovel just above his upper lip?' Roger asked.

Olrik replied, 'That's exactly what it is — a shovel. He uses it to push the snow out of his way so he can get at the lichen underneath. For most of the year lichen is his only food.'

'What is lichen?'

'It's something that will grow where nothing else will grow. It doesn't even have to have soil. It will grow on rocks. It's sometimes called reindeer moss because it's a little like moss, and all members of the deer family including the caribou consider it a good food. It keeps on growing even under snow. It never grows large, not over a few inches. Some Eskimos eat it — I've eaten it myself. It's not half bad.'

'Dad told us to get one of these caribou,' Hal

reminded his brother. 'He said it was the best friend of the Eskimos. It gives them most everything they need. Their warmest blankets are caribou hide, and their shoes can be made of it because it's strong. Its blood makes a good soup. They cut open the stomach to get the moss — they think it's as lovely as cake. The caribou provides them with meat, cheese, clothes, tents, buckets and bedding. In northern Canada the caribou have been the chief support of Eskimos for thousands of years. Clothes made from caribou hide are as warm as toast. You've got this one feeling pretty good, so I think it's time to take it to the airport.'

The great animal, nine hundred pounds of bone and muscle, was led by the horns a mile to the airfield, where it was placed in a box-car. After a few more animals were added the box-car would be mounted on an airplane, which would then be called a skyvan and would take off on a night flight to Long Island.

6
Terrible Journey

The two Yanks and Olrik looked at the ruins of the snow house that Hal had so carefully built.

There was not one block of snow standing on another. The caribou had done a thorough job.

'Are you going to rebuild?' Olrik asked.

'After we come back,' said Hal. This was a surprise to Roger.

'Are we going somewhere?'

'I've been thinking about making a trip,' Hal said. 'Up on the ice cap. Now is a good time to do it. Tonight we'll just sleep out in the open in our nice, warm, caribou-hide sleeping bags. Tomorrow we'll hire ten dogs and a sledge and take off.'

'You don't need to hire anything,' said Olrik. 'You can use mine. Provided you let me go along with you.'

'We'd like nothing better than to have you with us,' said Hal. 'Of course we'll pay you.'

'Of course you won't,' said Olrik. 'We Eskimos don't do things that way. Friends don't pay each other.'

Hal saw there was no use in arguing. He knew Eskimo custom. If your friend did something for you,

you would do something for him. Hal already had an idea of what he would do for Olrik and his parents. He would build them a stone house so solid that nothing could pull it down. This Eskimo's family now lived in an igloo. Hal had seen stone houses in Thule. The chinks between the stones were filled with mud which froze solid and kept out the cold. The roof was made of the skins of wild animals all sewn together, and sod completely covered the skins. This layer of earth was about three inches thick and froze almost as hard as ice. In summer it thawed a little, just enough for grass and flowers to grow in it. And what you really had was a roof garden above your head.

But he wouldn't breathe a word of this to Olrik until it was almost time for them to leave Greenland.

During the night snow fell, but the boys were snug in their furry bags and drew the flaps over their heads. In the morning they were practically buried under four inches of snow. Olrik couldn't find them at first. He saw two mounds and cleared them away only to find large rocks. Then at a little distance he saw the snow move as if it were alive. He cleared it away as best he could and discovered two very lively and hungry boys.

They heard a yapping sound that told them the dogs and sledge were already there.

'The huskies are ready to go,' said Olrik.

'Why are they called huskies?' Roger asked.

Olrik explained. 'A husky man is one who is big and strong. So they call these dogs huskies because they are big and strong.'

They kicked off the snow that covered their

supplies and had a quick breakfast. Then they loaded the sledge with all that they would need, mainly food. Also they put on crates and cages for the animals they expected to find.

'Where do we sit?' Roger wanted to know.

Olrik grinned. 'You don't sit. You walk. Unless you get sick. In that case, you ride. But you can't expect the huskies to go so fast if they have to haul a big fellow like you.'

The harness for the dogs was made of strips of walrus hide. The huskies looked powerful. Every one of them weighed ninety pounds or more. Olrik said they were the finest in Greenland. They looked a little more wolf-like than most dogs.

The sledge was four feet wide. The runners were the long jawbones of the Greenland whale. Roger admired them. He saw the bottom of each one was covered with ice.

'How did that happen?'

'I made it happen,' said Olrik.

'How?'

'You turn the sledge upside down. Then you pour water on the bottom of each runner. It quickly turns to ice. The well-iced runners glide smoothly over ice or snow.'

'Do the huskies have to be fed three times a day?'

'Not on your life,' laughed Olrik. 'They are fed only once every two days.'

'But don't they get hungry?'

'They do. And it's when they're hungry that they run fast. If they are stuffed with food they slow down.'

'But how can we walk or run without sinking into the snow?'

'I saw you had skis. I have a pair also. We'll put them on and then we can get along as fast as the huskies do.'

'How quiet your dogs are. Even when they bark it's hardly a bark.'

'No,' said Olrik. 'They have only two ways of speaking. One is a growl, and the other is a howl.'

'A howl,' said Roger. 'That's what wolves do.'

'Right. And I wouldn't be surprised if there's a bit of wolf in every one of these huskies. That doesn't mean that they like wolves. They're deathly afraid of them. Wolves killed seven of my dogs — killed them and ate them.'

'I hope we don't meet any wolves,' said Roger earnestly.

'We probably will. But we won't worry about that now. Are you ready to go? Better wear your skis. I have mine here. Then we won't stumble along so badly in the snow.'

They took off for the great beyond. Roger's heart thumped with excitement. Even his big brother was thrilled to think of the adventures that awaited them. They were going to travel on the mighty ice cap. Under them would be ice not three inches thick as on a lake or ocean, not three feet thick, but two miles thick. It seemed impossible.

It was not easy to get from the lowland up to the ice cap. It did not slope gently down from high to low. Instead it ended in a steep cliff three hundred or four hundred feet high. To get up such a cliff with ten huskies and a sledge was impossible.

There were only a few places in all Greenland where the abrupt cliff gave way to an easy slope from low to high. Olrik knew where to find the nearest one. The huskies were happy, the humans enjoyed speeding along on their skis in the sparkling fresh air straight from the North Pole.

Suddenly Olrik said, 'Now you are on the ice cap.'

The wind had blown the snow away and their skies were sliding over ice but it was only two inches thick.

'Is this a joke?' Roger demanded.

'No joke,' said Olrik. 'This is the edge of one of the two greatest caps of ice in the world. The other is in Antarctica. Now all we have to do is go up and up and up. The famous ice cap is only a few inches thick here. We will keep going until it is two miles thick. If anyone wants to go back, now is the time to say so.'

Nobody said so.

The rise was so gradual that they could still ski.

They had followed a road through the low country, but now there was no sign of a road.

Roger asked Olrik, 'Why don't we go up one of the roads?'

Olrik answered, 'There's no road across the ice cap.'

'I can see that there's no road here. But there must be somewhere. How do people get from one shore of Greenland to the other shore?'

'There's no road anywhere. There will be some day. Then automobiles will stream across from one side to the other of the great ice cap. They will pull caravans, or perhaps they will live in motor homes. They will stop where they please and have all the comforts of home. That day hasn't come yet.'

'How about snowmobiles — like the ones we have in America?' Roger asked. 'Then you could go anywhere without roads.'

'I know,' said Olrik. 'I've been there and I've seen them. They are all right but I hope they don't come here soon. I like my friends, the huskies. And I'd rather have the peace and quiet of the dog team than the noise and stink of engines. Besides, if your gasoline or petrol or whatever you call it ran out where would you be? There's no place up here where you could get more. With dogs you don't have to worry. They don't run on gasoline. They eat only once in two days and they are always cheerful and eager. Besides, you can make friends with them and you can't do that with an engine.'

Poor Olrik. The time would come, and soon, when the old pleasant way of life would change.

Now they were going up a slope so steep that they had to remove their skis, put them on the sledge and walk.

It was a stiff climb but the huskies never hesitated. Olrik didn't seem to mind it, but Hal and Roger did a good deal of snorting and puffing. Even the brave dogs were tiring. Roger understood now why his dream of resting comfortably on the sledge and being pulled up the mountain was not practicable. For three hours they struggled on.

Now they were nearing the top of the great ice cap. It didn't look at all as Roger had imagined it.

41

He had expected that it would be perfectly rounded, as smooth as the top of an old man's bald head.

But instead it was all hills and holes. The holes were great cracks in the ice, sometimes forty feet wide and hundreds of feet deep. The hills were drifts of snow that had grown higher and higher under the strong winds so that they rose into the air anywhere from twenty to ninety feet high. The snow had turned to ice so that they looked exactly like icebergs, except that they were not floating in the sea but two miles up in the air on top of the Greenland ice cap.

'We can go around some of them,' Olrik said. 'But this one ahead is so long that we can't take the time to go around it. We'll simply have to climb over it.'

Olrik picked out the place where this mountain range of ice could be climbed. It looked impossible to the boys from Long Island. But the huskies were tackling it and set an example of courage for the other climbers.

Up they went, slipping, sliding, advancing two yards and falling back one, but keeping at it until they reached the peak.

Now, what a view they had! Away down there by the sea, was the city of Thule. Around them they could count seventy nunataks, which was what Olrik called the pyramids of snow and ice.

Judging by the position of Thule, Roger guessed the direction of the North Pole.

'It must be that way,' he said. 'Hal, what does your compass say?' Hal got out his compass. The needle didn't point to the North Pole. Instead, it pointed south-west.

'What do you make of that?' said Hal. 'This compass must have gone crazy.'

Olrik grinned. He thought that the crazy one was Hal, not the compass.

'You're forgetting something,' he said. 'A compass never really points to the North Pole.'

'Then what does it point to?' Hal demanded.

'To the Magnetic Pole.'

'I remember now. The earth is a sort of magnet or bowl of electricity. The electric centre is down there to the south-west. But if you were in New York and looked at the compass you would be so far away from both poles that the compass would give you a pretty good idea of due north.'

'But up here,' complained Roger, 'we just have to guess where the North Pole is. It seems to me we've got to do a lot of guessing. We have to guess whether it is morning, noon or night. Look at that silly sun. All summer it never goes up in the sky. And it never sets. It just goes round and round, low down all summer. And up here, summer is like winter.'

He shivered inside his thick caribou coat.

'Here it is June,' he said, 'and it's a sight colder here than in New York in February. Everything is the wrong way around.'

'Well,' laughed Hal, 'that's what makes it interesting. You wouldn't want to find Greenland just another New York.'

They went down the hill of ice and wound their way in and out and over the nunataks.

A bitter wind came up. Winds could be terrific on the ice cap. Down at Thule they were not so bad.

But two miles up winds could tear over the surface of the ice cap at more than 150 miles an hour.

Soon they were all chilled to the bone.

To make matters worse, it began to snow. But it was the strangest kind of snow the boys from Long Island had ever known. It did not come down in big flakes. The strong wind ground the flakes into a powder.

'We call it snow dust,' said Olrik.

Like dust, it got into the parkas that covered their heads, inside their fur coats, even into their sealskin trousers, into every pocket, into their boots, and, worst of all, into their eyes, and into their ears, and even their mouths if they dared to open them.

Roger was lagging behind. He was a strong boy but he couldn't keep up with his twenty-year-old companions. An especially strong gust knocked him over and he lay in the snow. Oh, how good it was to lie down. He didn't care if he never got up. He was dizzy, tired, and all his natural energy was whipped out of him by this awful wind.

Hal looked back. He could not see his brother because of the dense cloud of flying snow dust. He called, but the screech of the wind was stronger than his shout. He would have to go back and find his brother. That should be easy — he need only follow his tracks.

But he found no tracks. They had promptly been filled by snow. Now, which nunatak had they come around last? He wasn't sure. He was getting light-headed.

'Wait a minute, Olrik. We've lost the kid.'

Olrik was only a few feet away but did not hear

him. But Olrik saw him stagger. At once he reached out to help him.

'I can't see anything,' Hal said.

'I know. You're having a white-out.'

'What's a white-out?'

'It's a dizzy spell because wherever you look there's nothing but white — white on the ground, white in the air, and a white sky. It's all very confusing. Some people have gone crazy in a white-out.'

'Well, I can't go crazy because I've got to find my brother. If he's tumbled down in the snow, he may freeze to death. Which way did we come?'

'I'm not sure. Fact is, I'm having a bit of a white-out myself,' said Olrik. 'But I know who can find him.'

'Who?'

'The huskies.'

He turned the dog-team about. Perhaps they thought they were going home. They went back as they had come and stopped where Roger lay in the snow. He was unconscious.

Hal pushed and pulled the body. 'Wake up,' he said. There was no response.

Olrik was worried. 'Is he dead?'

Hal pulled off one of Roger's fur mitts and put his finger where the pulse should be. He could feel nothing. The hand was stiff with cold.

'I'm afraid he's gone,' said Hal.

'Perhaps not. He's so cold the circulation has stopped in his wrist. Try his temple.'

Hal put his finger on a point about an inch in front of the boy's ear. At first he felt nothing. His own fingers were so cold that even if there were a pulse he might not feel it. He put his hand inside his own coat and warmed it up. Then he tried again. He found a very slow, weak throb in his brother's temple.

'Thank the Lord,' he yelled. 'He's alive!'

'That's great,' cried Olrik. 'Too many have died up here. Let's wrap him up in a couple of caribou hides and put him on the sledge. He ought to warm up and wake up. Perhaps he won't — but we'll do our best.'

The boy was bundled up in a caribou skin with the fur side inside. Around this was wrapped another skin with the fur side outside.

'That's the way we do it to get the most warmth,' Olrik said.

The huskies, who had thought they might be going home, were turned about and the trip was continued.

For an hour Roger lay there without moving, his eyes closed. Then warmth and life seemed to steal through his body and he opened his eyes.

'What am I doing on the sledge?' he asked. 'Am I a piece of baggage?' He tried to throw off the covers.

'Just try to be baggage for a while longer,' Hal said. 'We almost lost you.'

'I don't remember anything,' Roger said. 'Get me out of here. The dogs have enough to pull without me.'

'Don't move,' said Hal. 'Just pretend you are the King of Siam and this is your golden chariot.'

'The storm is letting up,' Olrik announced. 'Already there's a bit of blue above. In half an hour we'll see the sun. Then we'll stop for lunch.'

'How can you tell when it's lunch-time?' Hal wondered.

'By my stomach,' said Olrik. 'I don't really know whether it'll be lunch-time or dinner-time or midnight. Anyhow, something inside me tells me that it's time to eat.'

7
Perils of the Ice Cap

They put up a tent. It was easier than building an igloo every time they stopped. The tent was not made of canvas. It was far better than that. Thick caribou hide with plenty of shaggy hair still on the outside would keep out the cold and would also shut out the sunlight in case they wanted to sleep. The floor was another caribou hide.

'How about the dogs?' Roger asked. 'Don't they have to be unharnessed?'

'No,' Olrik answered. 'The harness is very light — it won't bother them. If a bear came around and the dogs were not harnessed they might run away and we'd never see them again. Or they might gang up against the bear and kill it. You wouldn't want that to happen.'

'But won't they freeze to death if they can't run?'

'They know how to avoid freezing. Come and take a look at them.'

He took Roger around to the side of the tent. There Roger saw one of the strangest sights he had ever seen in his life.

What he saw was a great heap of dog flesh. The weary huskies had piled up on each other so that every one of them was kept warm by the dogs who pressed against him on both sides or the dogs beneath or above him.

'Pretty smart dogs to think of that way of keeping warm,' Roger said. He was about to enter the tent when Olrik stopped him.

'First get rid of your snow dust,' he said. 'It's all over you. You look like a ghost. If you go into the tent that way and start your little stove, the snow dust that covers you will melt and soak into your clothes. Then if you come out your wet clothes will freeze and you will be dressed in ice.'

All three began to brush off the snow powder that covered them, blow it out of their noses, take it out of their ears and eyes, dump it out of their pockets, and turn their pockets inside out.

It was only when they were free of the pesky snow dust that they dared enter the tent, light the small portable stove, and eat.

'All I want to do now is sleep,' Roger said. Hal and Olrik were quite willing to do just that. Hal was the only one who carried a watch. He took it out and looked at it. It had stopped. Whether he had banged it against some icy nunatak or some snow dust had gotten into it, there was no doubt that it was useless.

'Well, it doesn't matter what time it is,' Hal said. 'We're all tired — let's sleep.'

It was some seven or eight hours later that Roger woke and looked into the face of a polar bear. It had forced its head in between the flaps and seemed to be trying to decide which of these juicy morsels to eat first. Roger had no desire to be a bear's breakfast.

His yell woke up his two companions and they stared with horror and disbelief as the great beast forced its way into the tent.

Olrik felt guilty. He should have brought a gun. But Hal had told him not to because they were not killers.

But the polar bear is a killer and could not live if he were not. He must kill if he wants to eat. What do three non-killers do if they face a killer?

Hal picked up the heavy frying pan and prepared for battle. Before he could land this heavy weapon against the bear's nose, the unwelcome visitor turned into one who was very welcome. The monster went straight to Roger and rubbed its great furry head against the boy's shoulder.

'It's Nanook!' cried Roger. 'Put away the frying pan.'

The bear lay down beside Roger, gargling something that may have been his effort to say, 'Good Morning'. Roger put his arms around the great furry neck. Both boy and bear were very happy.

'How did he ever find us?' Roger wondered. 'Our tracks must have been covered with snow.'

Olrik explained. 'It takes more than snow to defeat a bear's sense of smell.'

'I didn't know we smelled as bad as that,' said Roger.

'Bad or good, it's all the same to the bear. Two things brought him to you. One was smell — the other was love.'

They fed the bear and then had some food themselves. The three of them went out — the four of them — the bear following Roger.

It was a sparkling morning — if it was morning. The sun was shining bravely. It had of course been shining all the time they were asleep. The thick tent-hides had kept out the light. Now there was no snow dust, no wind. The sky was a great dome of pure blue.

But there was one thing that bothered Roger. 'We're supposed to be after animals and we haven't seen one — except Nanook.'

'They were all in their holes during the storm,' Olrik said.

'I don't believe there are any animals up here. How could there be? There's nothing for them to eat — not a sprig of grass, not a leaf, nothing.'

'They don't need grass or plants,' said Olrik. 'They're all carnivores, meat-eaters.'

'Where do they get the meat?'

'By eating each other. The bear eats the wolf. The wolf eats the wolverine. The wolverine eats the fox, and so on. All these animals eat birds such as the auks, the barnacle goose, the pink-foot goose, the white-tailed eagle, the Greenland falcon, the snow bunting, the snowy owl and the raven. So, don't worry, there's plenty of food for everybody.'

'Well,' said Roger, 'I think they're pretty smart to find it.'

'You're right. I saw a fox hole near that nunatak. Come and see how smart the fox is.'

They walked over to inspect the home of the fox. The animal was not present.

'Look in there,' said Olrik. 'See that pile of birds?'

'They don't have any heads,' said Roger.

'Exactly. Even a fox can't eat heads. These are all

52

auks. The fox bites off all their heads and piles up the bodies in neat rows, covers them with gravel, and puts stones on top. Then, when winter comes, he has a fine supply of food to last him through the dark months.'

Roger was astonished. 'I thought animals didn't have enough brains to think about the future.'

'Some, like the fox, can plan ahead better than some people do,' said Olrik.

It was such a lovely day that it seemed nothing bad could possibly happen.

But then it did. There was a wild commotion on the other side of the tent. The boys ran to see what was going on. Three wolves were not eating birds for breakfast. They were attacking the dogs.

'But they wouldn't really kill the dogs, would they?' said Roger. 'After all, the huskies and the wolves are cousins.'

'A cousin can kill a cousin,' Olrik said. 'Last year wolves killed all seven of my dogs.'

Roger popped into the tent and came out with a pan. He started beating it loudly and sang. It was a sound the wolves had not heard before. With ears erect, they stared at the boy with the pan.

'See? They're scared. They'll run away,' cried Roger.

The wolves ran, but not away. They attacked the boy with the pan. They had meant to make the dogs their breakfast, but this two-legged nuisance seemed to have plenty of meat on him and would make a good meal.

Hal and Olrik rushed at the wolves, yelling at the top of their lungs. The wild animals did not seem to notice them. Their savage teeth dug into the face and hands of the boy and they began to tear off his clothing. The wolves were the great heavy polar variety and Roger, though strong, could not resist them. They pushed him down on the ice and he lay there, protecting his face with his hands.

Hal began to sing. That was a strange thing to do, but Hal had learned that wolves hate singing. But this time the wolves paid no attention to the song.

Then, around the tent, came the great Nanook. With a roar that seemed to shake the nunataks, he attacked the wolves. In quick succession he swatted all three and they fell in a heap. The swat of a polar bear's paw is quite as strong as that of a lion. A lion can kill with one blow, and so can the great bear of the north. Two of the wolves were dead, and the third went limping away, howling.

Would the bear eat the breakfast so conveniently placed before him? That would be only natural, but since Nanook had just had his breakfast he left the carcasses where they were to be buried by the next snowfall.

Hal helped Roger to his feet and took him into the tent. He applied antiseptic to the scratches on Roger's face, then covered them with tape. He bandaged the boy's hands. Roger did not wince or whine although he was in great pain.

He thought he was being an infernal nuisance to his companions. Yesterday they had been forced to put him on the sledge. Today he would refuse to be treated like a baby. His legs were all right. A scratch had closed one eye but he could see with the other.

He saw Olrik taking food supplies out of the tent and putting them in a pile covered with rocks large enough to keep off animals.

'Where do these rocks come from?' Roger asked. Olrik pointed to the high mountains far to the east. There was no ice on them since they were so far up in the air.

'Rocks keep falling from those mountains.'

'How do they get here?'

'You ought to know after yesterday. The terrific winds they have up here can move rocks a few inches every year. That isn't much — but give them thousands of years and they can travel great distances.'

'Why did you put all those tins of food under the rocks?'

'That's called a cache. A traveller across these wastes leaves a cache of food once in a while so that when he comes back the same way it will be waiting for him and might save him from starvation. We'll put down several more caches as we go along.'

'But will we be coming back exactly this way?'

'Very likely. That's because the dogs want to get home. They'll follow the same route they came by. That's husky intelligence.'

They took down the tent, folded it, and strapped it to the sledge. It was a fine day, although quite a bit below freezing. The sun stayed so low that it gave off very little heat. Everybody was happy, including the fifteen-year-old behind his plasters and bandages.

8
Thunder River

'I hear thunder,' said Roger, and he looked up at the sky. There was not a cloud in sight. The sky was one great vault of brilliant blue.

And yet Roger heard thunder, and so did Hal.

Olrik said, 'It's not up there. It's down below. Pretty soon you'll see what makes it. We're just coming to Thunder River.'

They arrived at what seemed to be the end of the world. They looked down a steep cliff several hundred feet to a rushing river. Its loud roar echoed against the cliffs. The noise was tremendous. The boys agreed that Thunder River was a good name for this frantic torrent.

'How do we cross that?' Hal asked. 'Is there a bridge?'

'No bridge,' was Olrik's answer.

'Then how?'

'Swim.'

'You're joking,' said Hal. 'Three of us plus the bear plus ten dogs and a sledge? Swim?'

Olrik said, 'You can swim, can't you?'

'Of course. But not in that.'

Four of the dogs had gone over the edge and were

suspended by their walrus-hide harness. They were whining pitifully and struggling so wildly that the rawhide lines that held them might break at any moment and drop them to the bottom of the abyss.

Olrik saved them by backing up the other dogs so that the ones hanging in space were also pulled up and away to safety.

Hal was bewildered. 'Where does all this water come from?'

'From far away to the south where it is warmer than it is here. This is melt water from that part of the ice cap.'

'Why doesn't it freeze over?'

'It's running too fast to freeze.'

'Well, what do we do now? Can we go around it?'

Olrik shook his head. 'That would take us hundreds of miles out of our way. No, we'll have to cross it.'

'But how do we get down this cliff?'

'We don't. We'll go along the edge until we find a slope that may lead us down.'

The three boys and Nanook did as Olrik suggested. They found a place where the slope was gradual enough for the dogs to go down while the boys held back the sledge to prevent it from sliding forward and breaking the legs of the huskies.

Now they were at the edge of the river. It was a roaring tumult of water. It rushed by like an express train. Its waves leaped many feet into the air.

'It's quite impossible,' Hal said. 'I suggest we turn around and go home.'

Olrik laughed. 'You don't really mean that. I suppose you can both swim?'

'Yes, but not in that,' said Hal once more.

'And the dogs can swim. And the best swimmer of all is the polar bear. So why not strip off your clothes and pack them inside the tent, where they'll keep dry.'

Hal still had his doubts. He knew that his young brother had been pretty well beaten up by the wolves. Would he be able to stand the beating he would get from the waves of this wild river?

'Let's get to it,' said Roger. He took off his clothes and stowed them away. Hal did the same and so did Olrik. As for Nanook, he didn't mind getting his overcoat wet.

Olrik drove the huskies into the wild turmoil of water and foam. The huskies swam as these brave animals were used to doing, and the sledge floated on the surface. Waves broke over it but did not penetrate the inside of the tent. Roger hung on to the tail of the sledge. He was battered, bumped and pummelled by the waves but never let go. Nanook swam beside him protecting him from the worst of the rushing waves.

Hal swam without hanging on. That was his mistake. As soon as he came out of a back eddy into the main current he was carried off like a leaf in a gale. In vain he tried to swim back up to the sledge. It was no use. He was being carried steadily down toward the ocean. He crashed against unseen rocks. The waves played with him as if he were a football. One wave tossed him to the next wave, and they all howled with glee. They were having a good time, but Hal was not. He looked back and saw that the rest of the company had all reached the other shore.

Hal was perhaps the best swimmer, except for Nanook. But now he was losing his nerve, getting short of breath, swallowing too much water.

He tried to reach either shore, but the central current was too strong and held him firmly in its grip.

His eyes began to cloud over and his head ached. A little more of this, and he would be finished.

Then he was aware that someone was beside him. Was it Olrik, or was it Roger?

It was Nanook. This magnificent swimmer of the animal world would save his life. He placed himself on the downstream side of the exhausted Hal, and with the boy's body pressed hard against him he swam to shore. Hal found himself dumped on a bank of gravel and it felt like a bed of roses. He lay there almost unconscious until Olrik and Roger came to help him to his feet. The bear stood in front of him, looking up at him. Hal weakly reached down and took the bear's right foot in his hand.

'Thank you, pal,' said the boy to the bear.

9
Frozen Whiskers

The boys put on their clothes. The dogs had done their work well. The contents of the sledge had been splashed a bit, but there was no serious damage.

Hal's voice rose above the thundering voice of the river, 'Imagine — a river on the ice cap! Are there any others?'

'Half a dozen,' said Olrik. 'They all come from the south, where the deep snow that falls on the ice melts quickly and is in a great hurry to get to the sea. Hal, I want to show you what you just missed.'

'What did I miss?'

'Sudden death.'

Olrik led them around a corner, and there was a sight that made Hal's blood run cold — a waterfall plunged down more than a hundred feet and created new thunder as it crashed on rocks below.

Said Olrik, 'You would have been mushed to a jelly on those rocks if Nanook hadn't got to you just in time.'

'Good old Nanook,' said Hal.

'I think this is a good place to put another cache,' Olrik said. 'We'll remember it's just above the water-fall.'

Again, food was stored under heavy rocks.

Five miles farther on another cache was made. 'That makes three,' said Olrik. 'Now if we run out of food we'll be sure to have some waiting for us in these caches.'

Even Olrik could be wrong. It was not going to be as easy as he thought.

The weather changed, as it suddenly does on the ice cap. The sun disappeared behind a cloud. Up came the wind. This time there was no snow dust, but something worse. This was an ice storm.

The boys had been tramping over broken ice. Now the wind swept pieces of ice into the air and they cut painfully into their faces. They even ripped holes in clothing. The wind howled like a wild beast. The dogs were whipped off their feet. The boys could hardly breathe. It was bitterly cold, but the great effort of fighting the storm made them perspire. Hal had not shaved since leaving the lowlands, and he had a short beard on his cheeks and chin. Sweat covered his face and promptly turned to ice. Hal tried to wipe off the ice but did not succeed. Roger laughed as he looked at his brother.

'That's what you get for not shaving,' he said.

Hal tried to answer but his iced-over face was so stiff that he could not say a word. Even his lips were frozen together.

He took off his mitt and put his hand over his mouth in order to melt the ice. It didn't work, because his hand was frozen.

He had been told that his hands would unfreeze if he rubbed them in snow. That was fine. The only trouble was that there was no snow. There was nothing but these flying pieces of ice as sharp as fragments of a broken window. Like knives, they cut his face and the blood oozed out only to be frozen at once and make him look more wild than ever.

Roger had done what he saw Olrik do. Olrik had twisted his parka around so that it covered his face. Now he could not see, but he placed one hand on the crossbar at the back end of the sledge and trusted the dogs to keep going in the same direction. Roger imitated Olrik and got along pretty well.

However, Hal had one advantage. He was the only one who saw the small Arctic fox who stood gazing with wonder at the strange things that were passing him. Hal scooped it up and popped it into a crate on the sledge.

That was easy, but he didn't have as much luck when he tried to snatch a wolverine. It bit him viciously but his frozen hand didn't feel the pain. He managed to get hold of it and toss it into another crate.

The wolverine is a bunch of black hair with teeth. It is very cunning and cruel. It has no friends. If it is caught in a trap, it will run away and carry the trap with it. The Eskimos are superstitious about it. They think it is an evil spirit. They are afraid of it because it is so powerful and they try to get its power by wearing a bit of wolverine fur next to their skin.

It is about the size of a bulldog and looks a little like a black bear, though much smaller. It is believed to be the most powerful animal of its size in the world. There are great numbers of this little rascal in the Arctic. It finds food in places where no other

animal would look for it. It eats squirrels, hares, foxes, grouse, and birds when it can catch them. It lives in under-ice dens.

Hal had never seen one in a zoo and was sure that his father would be glad to have this unique beast to sell to some zoo-keeper who would appreciate such a strange animal.

Mr Frozen Face, the only one who could see, saw something else of great interest. He could not take care of this so quickly. He reached for the reins and stopped the dogs.

Olrik mumbled through his parka, 'What's up?'

'The best of luck,' said Hal. 'Four baby bears.'

There they were, four little fellows crowded close together to keep warm, and whimpering under the onslaught of flying ice. At a little distance was their mother, lying in the ice, stone dead.

A female polar bear usually has twins, but sometimes gives birth to quadruplets, four little bears.

These were exactly what Hal wanted because there was a great demand for polar bears. And it was good that they were small. Any zoo would rather have a small bear that would live for twenty-five years than a big bear whose life was nearly over.

Olrik and Roger lifted their parkas just enough to watch Frozen Face pick up the orphans, one at a time, and tenderly put them in a little house of their own. Because the bitter wind sang through the crate, he covered the small creatures with a caribou mat.

The wolverine in the next crate made a violent effort to get at these small balls of meat and fur, his favourite food, but he didn't succeed.

When the ice storm died down the tent was again erected, and after a sleep they planted a new cache of food to await their return journey. Hal's icy face melted and he once more looked like a human being instead of a pillar of ice.

10
Dance of the Hobgoblins

A strange thing happened that day. A black cloud blotted out the sun and yet light came from the sky.

A very strange light, with many colours, red, yellow, green, blue, grey and violet.

'What in the world is that?' Roger asked.

Olrik said, 'You are looking at what the dictionary calls the aurora borealis, but some Eskimos who never saw a dictionary imagine it to be a dance of hobgoblins.'

'What's a hobgoblin?' Roger wanted to know.

'It's something that doesn't exist — like a devil or an evil spirit. Many people are afraid of it. They think it means that they are going to have trouble.'

'We never saw this in Long Island.'

'No, you are not likely to see it anywhere except north of the Arctic Circle.'

What a show it was! Quivering rays of colour shot here and there. They bounced up and down as if they were dancing. They waved like a curtain blown by the wind. Every moment there was a change. Sometimes they wound about like a serpent.

Sometimes the colourful little devils danced around in a circle. Sometimes there was a faint whistling sound. It was all very weird and Roger shivered.

Hal said, 'You would think you were looking right up into heaven.'

'The Eskimos don't think of it that way,' said Olrik. 'Their heaven is not up in the sky — unless they have become Christians. The old Eskimo tradition is that heaven is down in the centre of the earth where it is nice and warm at all times. Hell is up in the sky. It is bitterly cold. It sends down freezing storms upon the earth. Many of man's troubles come from the sky. Terrible winds come from there. Hail, so big that people must go indoors to get away from it, comes from above. The devil called Thunder and the other devil called Lightning come from there. Even the sun refuses to go up there. If you have led a bad life you'll go up there when you die and you will freeze solid and stay frozen through all eternity. If you have led a good life you will go down to that lovely, warm, comfortable place beneath the earth and you will be cosy and happy for ever.'

Hal wished that he had a camera with a colour film, to make a picture of this wild dance of the sky devils. But he didn't think of them as devils. He knew that the whole performance was electrical and rarely seen anywhere except in the polar regions. Once in Long Island he had noticed a white glow in the northern sky but there was no red, blue, green and so forth in it, and no dance of the hobgoblins. After all, to see some of the world's greatest performances you had to go to this savage land of ice and snow.

11
Musk-Ox in Evening Dress

'I think we can go on for about another five sleeps,'
said Olrik. 'Then we'll turn around and go back.'

Roger was puzzled. 'Five sleeps! I suppose you
mean five days.'

'Well, I could hardly say that,' said Olrik, 'since
we have only one day all summer long. The Eskimos
don't count in days. They count the number of times
that they sleep. They sleep when they are tired. But
it's always daytime. The sun never quite sets until
summer is over. The whole summer is just one day.
But whenever we feel we have had enough we put
up our tent and sleep.'

'Why do you figure on five sleeps?'

'Because then our food will be almost gone. We
will have just enough to get back to the last cache
we set up. That was the fourth cache we made.
There will be food enough there to carry us on to
the third cache. What we get there will take us to
the second cache. And then the first cache, and after
that, Thule.'

So they set out to do five more 'sleeps' before turning back toward home.

'How's that hand of yours?' Olrik asked Hal.

'Still frozen solid,' Hal said. 'It doesn't hurt a bit. I know it'll hurt like fury when it starts warming up. I kept it out of the sleeping bag to keep it frozen so that I could get some sleep.'

'It mustn't stay frozen too long,' said Olrik, 'or the rot called gangrene will set in and you'll have to have your hand amputated.'

The idea that his hand might have to be chopped off was not pleasant. Hal knew that a good snow rub was necessary. But as far as the eye could see there was nothing but ice.

Olrik looked at the sky. 'Cheer up. Pretty soon it's going to snow.'

It did snow before sleep time. Hal promptly gave his hand the snow treatment. He would have preferred to keep it frozen, because then it didn't hurt. Now it began to give him terrible pain.

'Good,' said Olrik. 'That means circulation is coming back. The blood is beginning to flow down into your hand.'

'I don't understand it,' Hal said. 'Snow is cold, and yet it is warming my hand.'

'Snow is not as cold as it seems,' Olrik said. 'Animals like to be covered by snow. They burrow into snowbanks to keep warm. When our dogs lie in a heap they are happy if they are buried in snow.'

When Hal found that he could move his fingers, he discontinued the snow bath and tucked his aching hand under his caribou jacket, where it could get the heat from his body. Here it gradually stopped

hurting and felt like a hand once more, not a chunk of ice.

They travelled on for three sleeps, then came upon a treasure.

'A musk-ox!' exclaimed Olrik. 'There used to be a lot of them in Greenland. Most of them have been killed, so now they are extremely rare. We are in luck.'

The amazing thing about the musk-ox was its great coat of shaggy hair, hanging so low that it almost touched the ground.

'It reminds me of Mother,' Roger said.

'Is that any way to speak of your mother?' Hal protested.

Roger explained. 'Whenever Mom went out to a

party or a concert, she wore a long evening dress that reached all the way down to her feet.'

Olrik laughed. 'You have a good imagination, Roger, if you can compare this beast to your mother.'

'But what's the use of all that hair?'

'It's a lot better than a lady's evening dress,' said Olrik. 'It keeps the animal warm even when the temperature is way down below zero. It really consists of two coats — two heavy layers, and inside them there is a lovely undergarment of beautiful wool softer than cashmere. And there's one other thing the long evening dress is good for. If the musk-ox has a baby it can conceal the youngster behind those heavy curtains of fur.'

Hal sniffed the air. 'What's that strange smell?' he asked. 'It's not a bad smell and it's not a good smell. What is it?'

'Musk,' said Olrik. 'The lady is not only wearing evening dress, she is using perfume.'

'Well,' said Hal, 'it doesn't exactly smell like perfume.'

'Perhaps not,' said Olrik, 'but the manufacturers of perfume couldn't get along without it. In almost every bottle of perfume there is some musk.'

'Do they get it only from the musk-ox?'

'No — some other animals secrete musk — the civet, musk-rat, otter, and the musk-deer.'

The musky musk-ox showed no inclination to run away. Instead it acted as if it might charge at any moment. It tossed its great head around, made threatening grunts, and lowered its curved, sharp-pointed horns dangerously.

'But I'm sure the lady would be too much of a lady to attack us,' Roger said.

'Don't be too sure,' said Olrik. 'It happens that this lady is no lady. This is a bull. He would like nothing better than a fight and he could kill us all in a few minutes.'

The bull was angrily pawing the ground.

Hal didn't wait to be flattened under that quarter-ton of wild beast. He drew his sleep gun from the sledge and sent a dart into the animal's neck. The medicine in one dart was not enough to put the beast to sleep but at least it would calm him down. The bull turned and began to wander away. Hal's lasso whistled through the air and the loop settled over the great head just behind the horns. Hal fastened the end of the line to the sledge and Olrik snapped the long whip over the dogs. The ten huskies began to pull and the musk-ox, half asleep, staggered along behind.

After five sleeps they all turned about and headed for home.

They got one more fine animal — a wandering reindeer. This was a polar reindeer, quite different from the reindeer of Lapland. It did not bite them and was easily captured. It was graceful and beautiful. Unlike the musk-ox it had no curtains reaching to the ground. Its body was well formed and its horns were magnificent. This was a male. The female also has horns, but not so large.

'You judge reindeer antlers by the number of points,' said Olrik. 'I've made a careful count and find there are sixty points in this animal's fine set.'

'Does the reindeer have any enemies?' Roger asked.

'It doesn't like wolves,' Olrik answered. 'And its worst enemy is the raven.'

'How can a raven do any harm to a big reindeer?'

'It swoops down and pecks out its eyes.'

'You said the animals on the ice cap live by eating other animals,' Roger said. 'But I don't believe the musk-ox and reindeer eat other animals. So how do they live on the ice cap?'

'They scratch away the snow from the rocks and eat the lichens that grow on them.'

Like the musk-ox, the reindeer was attached by a long line to the sledge and walked along behind.

Click, click, click went his feet.

'What's all the clicking about?' Roger asked.

Olrik answered, 'The bones in the reindeer's feet rub together and make that noise. All the little animals hear that sound and get out of the way. I don't know of any other animal on earth that clicks as he walks along. There's one other way that the reindeer is different. He has flat feet as big as pancakes.'

'I'm getting hungry,' said Roger.

'We're all out of food,' Olrik said, 'but we don't have to wait long. As soon as we get to the first cache we can eat.'

12
Starving Is No Fun

After the last sleep there had been no breakfast. There would be no lunch. Some hours later they should get to the cache.

The dogs ran twice as fast as usual because they were going home. But even this was not fast enough for the stomachs of the hungry boys. Then Roger had an idea.

'Don't reindeer pull sledges in Lapland?'

'So I've heard,' Hal said.

'Well, we have a reindeer. Why can't he pull instead of being pulled?'

Olrik said, 'I should have thought of that. Hal, you have a bright kid brother.'

He stopped the team. The huskies were not harnessed two by two as in Canada where the whole outfit must be narrow to get through the trees. On the ice cap there were no trees — so the dogs were spread out in a sort of fan. Each dog could see straight ahead instead of having nothing to look at but the rear of the dog in front.

The reindeer was brought around and placed in the middle of the fan, five dogs on one side of him and five on the other.

Then Olrik cracked his whip and away they all went like the wind. The boys could not run so fast, so they climbed on to the sledge.

This did not slow things down in the least. The reindeer was so strong and swift that he was almost equal to all the dogs put together.

The musk-ox kept up well in spite of the wind that caught his side curtains and sent them flying up in the air.

As for the great thousand-pound bear, he could have been excused for being slow because of his weight. But he was not slow. All his life he had been forced to run if he wanted to eat. Even now he stopped for an instant to put his teeth into a lemming, and again to catch an Arctic hare, yet he at once regained his place beside the rushing sledge.

So it was not surprising that they came in sight of the cache sooner than they expected. The boys shouted and the dogs howled. Soon they would fill those aching stomachs.

But as they came nearer, Olrik began to worry. The stones he had put over the food had been disturbed. Something or somebody had been tampering with the cache.

He hauled his team to a stop beside the cache.

It was empty.

Not one scrap of food remained.

'Look,' said Hal. 'Aren't those bear tracks?'

'That's just what they are,' said Olrik, 'and the tracks go that way.'

Nanook was sniffing the tracks. Then he began to follow them. Behind a big clump of ice he found the thief.

At once there was a battle royal. The other bear was as big as Nanook. But he was loaded down with food and his reactions were slow. Nanook gave him a thorough lambasting, tearing out his fur, bloodying his nose, biting off his tail.

But that didn't get the food back. Roger called Nanook. His huge pet came at once. The other bear stumbled off. He had been taught a lesson. He would think twice before robbing another cache.

Olrik, who was as hungry as the others, tried to be cheerful.

'Never mind,' he said. 'Let's hope we have better luck at the next cache.'

But when they arrived at the spot they saw wolf tracks all about. A pack of wolves had been here. However, the stones still stood up, so the food must be under them.

Then Olrik noticed that just one stone low down had been pulled away. The hole was big enough for wolves, one at a time, to crawl in and steal their dinner.

He pulled down the other stones and saw that all the supplies had vanished.

Hal and Roger could have stormed at Olrik for not building better caches. They didn't. They knew that Olrik had done his best, and now he was just as hungry and unhappy as they were.

'Sorry,' said Olrik.

'Not your fault,' said Hal.

Having eaten nothing, they were even more weary than usual. So they put up their tent and went supperless to their sleeping bags.

The animals did better. The dogs, the musk-ox and the reindeer all scraped away the snow and ate the lichen that grew on rocks.

Roger heard them scratching and chewing, and crawled out to see what was going on.

Lichen! They were all eating lichen. It must be good.

He scraped away some of it and put it in his mouth. It was bitter. Manfully, he swallowed it. His indignant stomach threw it up. It would rather be empty than try to digest such fodder.

Roger thought he would have some fun with his brother and Olrik. After sleep he said, 'You don't need to be hungry any more. You've got tasty food all around you.'

'What do you mean?' demanded Hal.

'Lichen. It's on the rocks. You'll love it. Just try it.'

They were hungry enough to try anything. Their faces twisted as they tasted the bitter lichen. They swallowed it, and up it came.

Hal glanced at Roger. 'You son of a gun. If I

weren't so weak I'd wallop you so hard that you couldn't stand up.'

'I'm glad you're weak,' said Roger.

Surely, by the time they reached the cache above the waterfall, their bad luck would turn to good. But a crack between the stones was just large enough to admit an Arctic fox. His tracks as he came were light, and heavy as he left loaded down with a good meal.

Now they had to cross Thunder River. The reindeer was unhitched. Roger had said he wanted to ride it.

'You'll both sink,' said Olrik. 'You and the reindeer.'

But Roger remembered what he had read about reindeer. Every hair of the reindeer was hollow and was full of air, which meant that the reindeer couldn't sink even if he tried. His body was so high out of the water that Roger rode across without getting wet.

Hal and Olrik put their clothes inside the waterproof tent. Olrik drove the dogs and sledge across, and Hal swam.

The line that held the musk-ox broke and the beast in his heavy evening dress was swept down toward the falls. If he went over the waterfall he would be killed on the rocks below.

The best swimmer of all, Nanook, gripped one end of the trailing dress and swam against the strong current to the other shore. The bewildered musk-ox clambered out on the sand, making his own waterfall as the river water poured out of his masses of shaggy fur.

The dogs were used to going without food for many sleeps, but the boys slept the sleep of utter exhaustion.

Feeling more dead than alive, they lay on the sledge until the final cache was reached. Here there were no animal footprints. But there were human prints, of heavy boots. And the cache was empty.

Somebody had stolen the food. How could any man be so mean? Whoever it was could be charged with murder if one of the starving boys fell dead.

Nothing was left in the cache except a slip of paper. Hal picked it up. It was a picture of Zeb. Zeb was in the habit of carrying a bunch of pictures of himself and handing one out to anybody he met. He had dropped this one by mistake.

The boys went on to Thule, where they made straight for an eatery.

'Don't eat too much,' Hal warned them. 'Our stomachs aren't used to food. They'll just throw it up, unless you eat very little. A couple of hours later, you can eat a little more. After another hour, some more. Take it easy, or you'll have trouble.'

They felt like devouring everything in the place, but they followed Hal's advice and went easy. Then they had food put up for them to eat later.

Off to the airfield to put their haul of animals into the box-car. The snow-white Arctic fox, the wolverine, the four small polar bears, the great musk-ox, the beautiful polar reindeer. The airport hands slid the box-car on to the flat deck of the skyvan and Hal wired his father to expect the shipment.

Not until this was done did they think of making

a home for themselves. They went back to the ruins of their igloo and began building a new one.

Zeb strolled over, not to help, but to look on.

'What did you do that for?' said Hal.

'Do what for?' said innocent Zeb.

'Steal everything in that cache.'

'You're out of your head,' Zeb replied. 'I don't know anything about any cache.'

'Oh, you don't? How about this picture?' He pulled out Zeb's photograph.

'Well, what's the matter with that?' said Zeb. 'It's a pretty good picture of me, isn't it?'

'Yes, it is,' said Hal. 'It's the picture of a thief and a killer. I picked it up in the cache. You should be arrested for attempted murder. But since you're only a half-wit, we'll just give you a good spanking.'

'Spank me?' yelled Zeb. 'Do you think I'm a baby?'

'That's just what we think. Heave ho, boys.' And all three, Hal, Roger and Olrik, grabbed Zeb, laid him face down over a snowbank, and gave him such a hard beating that Zeb would never forget it as long as he lived.

13
The Man Who Ate His Foot

'What did he do?'

The question was asked by one of the Eskimos who had gathered to see the spanking.

'Just tried to kill us,' Hal said. 'Stole our food from the cache.'

'He should go to prison for that.'

'He doesn't know any better,' said Hal.

'Empty up here?' said one man, tapping his head.

Hal nodded. He noticed that the Eskimo who had just spoken was on crutches. One foot was gone.

'What happened to your foot?'

'I ate it.'

'You're joking,' said Hal.

'It was no joke,' replied the Eskimo, a fine-looking fellow, strong, and taller than most of his people. 'You know what a bad place it is — up there on the ice cap. I went for days without one scrap of food. My right foot froze solid. There was no feeling in it at all. I couldn't give it the snow rub — the wind had blown away the snow. If I didn't do something, gangrene would crawl up my leg and kill me. So I took my snow knife and chopped off my foot.'

'Wasn't that very painful?'

'I didn't feel it at all. All I knew was that I would die if I didn't get something to eat. So I ate my foot.'

'I don't blame you,' said Hal. 'My hand froze. If there hadn't been snow to warm it I might have done what you did. By the way, where did you learn English?'

'In school. We had to learn Danish and English.'

'And the Eskimo language?'

'We learned that from our parents.'

'So you speak three languages!' said Hal. 'You're way ahead of me. I speak only one.'

'What's your name?' he asked, forgetting that an Eskimo never gives his name. A man close by said, 'His name is Aram.'

Hal shook hands with Aram. 'What do you do now?'

Aram said, 'I teach in the school that used to teach me. I'm lucky. I get a good salary and my folks are rich. All I lack is one foot.'

There was one thing a man on crutches could not do. He could not help build an igloo. Hal had been working while talking and with the aid of Olrik, Roger, and the Eskimos, the new snow home was ready for use.

'Aram, you will be our first guest. Come into our palace.'

Roger went in with them, but Olrik said, 'You must excuse me. I've got to get my dogs home and feed them.'

Hal, Roger and Aram sat down on the double

thickness of caribou hide that covered the ground. How good it was, after all the danger and agony of the desert of ice over which they had travelled.

'Many people have starved to death up there,' Aram said.

Hal said, 'The only food we found was lichen, and we couldn't keep it down.'

'I know a man', said Aram, 'who ate his trousers, made of caribou hide. And another who ate his seal-skin mittens. And two men who had to eat their dogs. And one who ate his sleeping bag. And a party ate the walrus hide that they had wrapped around the runners of their sledge. And one ate his boots, and went on barefoot over the ice until his feet froze. And two men ate the fleas and lice that they picked off their dogs. And one ate his own clothes made out of animal skins. And one kept alive seven days by eating those little animals you call lemmings, along with leather scraps and bones.'

'How could anybody eat bones?' Roger asked.

'You should try it some time,' said Aram. 'It can be done if your teeth can stand it. Inside the bones there is marrow and it is good food. If you can't break the bones with your teeth you can crush them between two rocks.'

'I ate a couple of mice,' said Hal, 'but I didn't like them any more than they liked me.'

'You were lucky', Aram said, 'that your dogs didn't eat each other.'

'They weren't quite that hungry', Hal said, 'because we cut up a walrus hide into pieces so small that they swallowed them without chewing. I had heard that they lie in the stomach for days before they are completely digested. So the dogs did a little better than we did.'

'If you eat your dogs,' said Aram, 'you are apt to come down with a disease called trichinosis and it will kill you.'

'That's the last thing we would do, eat our fine huskies,' said Hal.

Aram said, 'Another thing that can kill you is sweat. Running along, you are apt to sweat. The sweat turns to ice. Your whole body is encased in ice like a suit of armour. At first it's painful. Then it becomes comfortable and you get drowsy as the circulation of your blood slows down. And then you die.'

Hal said, 'Aram, what would you say is the most dangerous thing on the ice cap? Is it the bear, or the wolf, or what?'

'No,' said Aram. 'The most dangerous thing is man. Many crimes have been committed on the ice cap. There are no police up there. The fellow called Zeb nearly finished you off.'

Hal laughed. 'Well, he didn't succeed. And I'll bet his backside feels so bad now that he's sorry he tried. Now, let me serve you something a little better than mice, lice and old boots.'

He took a pan from the little stove and filled three bowls with a rich, delicious soup he had bought at the Thule eating place.

They relaxed in the cosy igloo and Hal murmured, '*Home, Sweet Home.*'

14
Ghosts Get Angry

Aram took them to see his parents.

'They are very good people,' he said, 'but you mustn't mind their old-fashioned ideas. They never went to school. They live in the farthest north where people have not changed their ways in a thousand years.'

Hal and Roger went with him to the airport, where Aram kept a small plane. Boarding it, they flew past Thule and on to the shore of the polar sea. There was nothing between this land and the North Pole.

Here, at the edge of the world, the igloos were better built. Farther south the art of igloo building was dying out since so many Eskimos now lived in stone and sod houses.

Aram took them to a beautifully built igloo with a large window made of a sheet of transparent ice.

The boys were warmly received by Aram's father and mother. They did not speak English, but Aram translated everything they said.

'An old man is happy that you have come to see him,' said the father.

Roger was puzzled. He asked Aram, 'Who is the old man he speaks about?'

'Himself,' said Aram. 'Eskimos are very modest. They think it is rude to say 'I' or 'me'. So they speak as if they were talking about someone else.'

The mother spoke and her voice was very low and sweet.

'My mother,' said Aram, 'wants you to know that an old woman is surprised that you have come so far to see people who are not worth bothering about. And she asks if you would like some fresh blubber. Say yes.'

Hal nodded and smiled. 'Tell her that her visitors would be delighted to have some fresh blubber.'

Roger objected. 'Hey, what are you getting us into? Blubber is the fat that animals up here have under their skin to keep out the cold. Who wants to eat a chunk of stinking fat?'

'You do, tough guy,' said Hal. 'Be polite, or we'll kick you out. Smile and bow.'

Roger smiled and bowed. He didn't do it too well. He took the blubber and tried not to wrinkle his nose in disgust as he swallowed the greasy stuff as quickly as possible.

Aram's mother was delighted. She said gently, 'An old woman who is no good would be proud to have a son like this one. He is half Eskimo already.'

The father said, 'An old man thinks you must be very happy to get away from your country where it is so hot and there is no snow for a sledge.'

Roger wanted to say, 'Baloney!', but Hal replied, 'Yes, in New York all summer we don't have one bit of snow. And it's so hot we have to turn on what we call "air conditioning" to cool the house.'

The old folks shook their heads sadly. Father said, 'An old man thinks you were very lucky to come here. In your country you don't even have the North Pole.'

Hal said, 'I've heard that the Eskimos never punish their children. How do you make them behave? Surely you spank them once in a while.'

The old man turned to Aram. 'Were you ever spanked?'

'Never,' said Aram. 'Perhaps I should have been.'

'No,' said the old Eskimo. 'Striking a child just puts an evil spirit into him. The air is full of evil spirits trying to get into us.'

'He means ghosts,' Aram smiled. 'The Eskimos believe that everyone who dies becomes a ghost and tries to do mean things to the living. If anyone gets sick, it's an evil ghost that is making him sick. So they think. There is no doctor up here — only the medicine man. He sells you all sorts of things that are supposed to keep off the ghosts. Perhaps they will show you some of them.'

He spoke to his parents. At once they began to lay out all the things they had bought from the medicine man — they called him a shaman — and the boys were bewildered by the vast numbers of things that the shaman had insisted they must have to keep off bad ghosts.

A seal's eye to fend off the evil eye.

A rabbit fur against frostbite.

A bear's claw to keep off the evil spirit called lightning.

An ermine's tail against the wild dance of devils in terrible storms.

A caribou tooth to avoid starving. ('Just what we needed when we had no food,' said Hal.)

The paw of a wolverine to keep you from going crazy.

The head of a fox so no-one could play tricks on you.

The ear of a deer so you could hear well.

The skin of a lemming against sickness.

And many more.

Surely the cloud of ghosts that were supposed to fill the igloo had no chance to do harm so long as they were held off by all these ghost-stoppers.

No wonder the shaman got rich, selling these worthless objects to people who trusted him and believed everything he said.

'Every month when the moon is great,' said the

old man, 'the shaman goes up to see the man in the moon who will tell him what to do next.'

The mother gathered up a large pan of food. She said, 'An old woman will take this to our neighbour, who has nothing to eat.' She went out, and came back presently with an empty pan.

When had the boys from Long Island seen anyone take a good dinner to a neighbour?

Never.

No matter how ignorant these people were, their hearts were true and kind.

They would not let the boys go without feeding them well. Meat was served to each of them. It was raw and it was rotten. And it smelled.

The mother said, 'We have been keeping it a long time. Now it is ripe and ready to eat. Some white people cook it. That spoils it. An old woman hopes you will like it.'

Roger's stomach almost threw up its blubber. The odour of the rotten meat made him want to hold his nose. His hand started to go up, but Hal caught it in time.

'It won't kill you,' he said. 'Eat it, and like it.'

'I'll bet you're not going to eat yours.'

'Watch me,' said Hal.

He put a gob of it in his mouth. His face took on an expression of utter agony. He sneezed, and his delicious meat sprayed out all over the caribou floor. The old woman at once cleaned it up, and put it back on Hal's plate.

Roger laughed until he thought he would burst.

Hal began to apologize. 'It's nothing,' said the mother, Aram interpreting. 'You're just not used to it. I did the same thing when someone gave me cooked meat.'

Hal and Roger downed the meat. It stayed down. They were very proud of themselves.

A young man came in. He seemed very unhappy. 'Something awful has happened. My wife had a baby.'

'Is that awful?' Aram's mother said.

'No. The awful thing is this — the baby has no teeth. It's our first baby. Should we throw it away? How can it eat without teeth?'

'Your wife will nurse it,' said Aram's mother.

'But it would be bad for it to grow up without teeth. I think we will throw it into the sea. Perhaps the next baby we have will have teeth.'

He was just going out when the old man called him back.

'I don't think you understand,' he said. 'Look at Aram. He had no teeth.'

'No teeth? It's strange that he is still alive. How does he get along without teeth?'

'He has teeth now. Show him your teeth, son.'

Aram bared his teeth.

'How did he get them?' said the worried young father. 'Some people put caribou teeth in their mouth.'

'Those didn't come from any caribou. And he didn't have them when he was born. But they grew up later.'

'That doesn't make sense. You're just trying to comfort me. Our baby wasn't born without hands. He wasn't born without a nose, or without ears. He has legs, and ten toes. He's all there — except teeth.

That's bad — and you can't tell me it's good. I think I'll dump the brat.'

'You'll do no such thing,' said Aram's mother. 'Just be patient. The teeth are there, but they haven't come up yet. Give them time. It's your wife you should be thinking about just now — not your baby. I will go and see if she is all right.'

She looked at Hal and Roger. 'I'm sorry. Perhaps you will come again.' And she was gone.

15
Flight to the North Pole

Hal looked out through the ice window to the polar sea.

'Just think,' he said, 'the North Pole is right over there.'

'I can't see it,' said Roger.

'Neither can I. It's seven hundred miles away. Peary spent years trying to get across that 700-mile stretch by dogteam. He didn't get there until 1909. The first man to get to the North Pole.'

'Now you can get there in two hours,' said Aram.

'You don't mean it,' Hal said. 'No dogs could cover seven hundred miles in two hours. Besides, the sea is all broken up by drift ice. And there are wide lanes of water between the floes.'

'Floes?' said inquisitive Roger. 'What are floes?'

'You're looking at them,' said Hal. 'Those pieces of floating ice are called floes.'

Roger saw one that was as flat as a raft and about twelve feet wide. 'Are they all like that?'

'Some are smaller. Some are much larger. I've heard of a floe that was as big as the state of Connecticut.'

'Gee!' exclaimed Roger. 'The North Pole right there and we can't get to it.'

'Yes you can,' said Aram. 'I'll take you.'

'You're kidding,' said Hal.

'No I'm not. Button up your caribou coat and come along. Next stop, North Pole.'

He led them out to his plane. They climbed in, still doubting that Aram could do what he promised.

Away they flew, over the floes and the open water between them, with no worry about dogs and sledges that had made the journey so difficult for Admiral Peary.

Within two hours they came down on a great expanse of ice.

'Meet the North Pole, gentlemen,' said Aram.

'But there's nothing here,' said Roger as he stepped down.

'And there never will be,' said Aram. 'There is no land under this ice — nothing but water fourteen thousand feet deep. What you are standing on is just a great ice floe. And like all floes it drifts.'

'But', said Hal, 'I understood that Peary planted a mast here with a flag to prove that he had reached the Pole.'

'Right,' said Aram. 'But the floe where he planted his mast and flag floated away. And another floe came, and another, and another. Floes are always on the move. The wind blows them along, or a current carries them. I suppose thousands of floes have passed over the Pole during the seventy years since Peary was here.'

'So there's been nothing here since Peary's time?'

'Oh yes, other people have tried. They can't get

it through their heads that nothing will stay at the North Pole. The Russians put a weather observatory here. It drifted away. Another expedition brought ten tons of building material and put up a station. When they came back, it was gone.'

'But there's a station at the South Pole and it doesn't float away,' said Hal.

'It can't move,' said Arám, 'because there is land beneath. Here there's just water.'

'Anyhow,' said Roger, 'it's great to be here on the very tip-top of everything. You just can't go any farther north than this.'

'Yes,' said Aram, 'this is the end of north. Nor is there any east or west here.'

'How do you make that out?'

'Well, just think a bit. There's no direction here but south. It's south to Greenland, isn't it? And it's south to Canada. It's south to Alaska. It's south to Norway. It's south to Great Britain. And that brings you back to Greenland — we will go south to get there. Anywhere you turn, you are looking south.'

A big plane roared overhead. It did not stop. 'Where's it going?' Roger wondered.

'It's a Japanese plane,' said Aram. 'It's going from Greenland to Japan. Our trading post buys a lot from Japan.'

'But why does it fly over the North Pole?'

'Because that's the shortest way. The trip around the world to Japan would be twice as long.'

'I can't imagine that,' said Hal. 'I'll have to look at a map.'

'A map won't help you,' said Aram. 'It's flat. The earth is round, like a globe. Drop in at my school.

We have a globe there. You can measure the distances — over the Pole, or around the earth.'

'So there's a lot of traffic over the Pole?'

'Dozens of planes every day.' Aram laughed. 'It's as busy as Times Square, or Fleet Street. And it's not just the planes that go this way. Since the submarine *Nautilus* passed under the North Pole in 1958, many subs do the same every year. Since the water is more than two miles deep, there is plenty of room under the ice for a sub to go full speed without bumping into anything more than a fish or two.'

'Or a whale or two,' laughed Hal.

'They don't come this far north,' said Aram.

There was a crashing sound as their floe was struck by other floes, hurled against it by the waves.

'I think we'd better get going,' said Aram, 'before this floe breaks up under us.'

He flew them back to their igloo. The next day Hal visited Aram's school and examined the globe. Aram was right. The shortest way to many lands was over the North Pole.

No longer was it a place of mystery. Many explorers had given their lives in the struggle to reach it. Without any effort, thanks to Aram, the boys had stood where Peary had stood, *on the top of the world*.

16
The Walrus Said . . .

'The time has come,' the Walrus said,
'To talk of many things:
Of shoes — and ships — and sealing-wax —
Of cabbages — and kings —
And why the sea is boiling hot —
And whether pigs have wings.'

So Lewis Carroll wrote about the walrus.

The Eskimos call it 'the sea horse'.

That makes two sea horses in the ocean. The walrus is one. The other is the little fellow two or three inches tall who always stands up on his hind feet and who has a head that looks exactly like the head of a horse.

The Eskimos also call the walrus 'The Old Man of the Ice Floes'.

And he does look like an old man as he sits on his floe, his tusks almost three feet long hanging straight down. At a distance, the white tusks look like a long white beard.

John Hunt had asked his sons to capture a walrus. To do this it was necessary to use a kayak.

'What's a kayak?' Roger asked his big brother.

Big Brother knew a lot, but he had never been in a kayak.

'It's a sort of canoe,' Hal said. 'But it's quite different from the canoes that we have used for hundreds of miles in our travels. It's not made of wood like the canoe. There's hardly any wood in north Greenland — so they use sealskin.'

'What good is that? Couldn't a walrus punch a hole in it with one of his tusks?'

'You guessed it. That's a risk we have to take. If that happens, I'll meet you at the bottom of the sea.'

They hired two kayaks. The owner told the boys how to use them. 'A kayak takes one person only. You notice that all the top of it is covered except for one hole where you get in.'

'It's as good as a canoe,' Roger said.

'It's a lot better than a canoe. If a canoe upsets, you drown unless you are a good swimmer. If a kayak upsets, you just flip it back up and you are not even wet.'

'How come? How can you go upside down and not get wet?'

'You wear this sealskin coat. No water can get through it. The hood is watertight. The collar fits tightly around your neck. The sleeves are tight-fitting. Best of all, the lower edge of the sealskin fits into this ring around the manhole so that not a drop gets into the kayak even if it is upside down.'

'That's wonderful,' Hal admitted. 'But if you are upside down, how do you get right side up again?'

'You must hang on to your paddle. One stroke of the paddle, and up you come.'

'Great,' said Roger. 'I can't wait to try it.'

Hal was anxious about what might happen to his eager brother.

'Take it easy,' he said. 'Watch me. I'll try to do it right and you copy me.'

The kayaks were only ten feet long and far lighter than any canoe they had ever carried around a waterfall or rapids. They carried them over their heads to the water's edge, launched them, and carefully stepped in, making sure to lock themselves into the ring around the manhole so no water could get into the kayaks.

Then they paddled off, searching for 'The Old Man of the Ice Floes'.

Usually a walrus hunter carried a harpoon, since his purpose was to kill the beast. But the boys had a much harder job. Their father would have no use for a dead walrus. They must take it alive. Each boy carried a lasso.

The Eskimo owner of the kayaks stood on the shore watching the boys hunting for a 3,000-pound walrus with nothing but two pieces of rope.

'They are just like children,' he thought. 'We Eskimos are much wiser than these children from the hot lands.'

And the 'children from the hot lands' considered themselves far better than the ignorant folk of the Arctic. Who was right? It was hard to say.

Hal had his doubts about this adventure. To take a walrus with a rope was like trying to catch an elephant with a piece of string.

Finding a walrus was the easy part. There were dozens of them, each on a cake of ice, singing their hearts out. Well, not exactly singing. The sound

was more like the bellow of a bull or the bark of a bloodhound. Anyhow, it tore the air apart with noise.

As the kayaks came near, they slid off their icy pedestals and disappeared under water.

'They're all gone,' said Roger.

'Never mind. They have to come up to breathe.'

'How long can they stay down?'

'About nine minutes.'

'What do they do down there?'

'Use those sharp tusks to dig up the bottom for shellfish.'

'Do they swallow them, shells and all?'

'No. I've read that they crush the clam shells between their flippers, then drop the pieces of shell and eat the clam.'

'But clam shells and oyster shells are like iron. How could they break them with a pair of flabby fins?'

'Not so flabby,' said Hal. 'A walrus could take your head between its fins and turn it into a pancake.'

'It must be as strong as a horse. No wonder they call it a sea horse. How deep does it go? Thirty feet?'

'More like three hundred feet. A man is apt to get the bends if he goes down a hundred feet without a scuba. The walrus does three times as well. But if he doesn't come up for breath, he dies. Watch. Here they come now.'

Up they came, poking their black heads out of the water and whistling a tune as they inhaled — not once, but a dozen times until every crevice of their lungs was full of air.

They were annoyed to find the kayaks still there and roared their disapproval. A big bull charged Hal's kayak and upset it. Hal forgot what he had told Roger not to forget. Surprised by this sudden attack, he let go of his paddle. It was a strange feeling, his head hanging three feet under water, as he held his breath, paddling desperately with his hands to turn the boat upright.

It didn't work. His hands were not as good as a paddle. He groped about but could not find it. He was getting dizzy. He could not hold his breath any longer. What a way to die, upside down!

But if there was any dying to be done he was glad that he was to do it, not his kid brother.

What was the kid brother doing all this time?

He had brought his kayak up beside Hal's and was trying to roll Hal's boat over. He couldn't budge it. Hal's weight kept it down.

Hal was a good swimmer. But he was locked into the kayak. Roger realized that a kayak, however good, had its drawbacks. Once in it, it was a devil of a job to get out of it.

Hal's paddle was drifting away. Roger passed his paddle down. It poked Hal in the ribs and woke him from his stupor. He grabbed the paddle, and with one stroke he turned his kayak and himself right side up. Roger captured Hal's drifting paddle.

The bull had been waiting for his chance to make trouble. He was more than the usual length of twelve feet. Some bulls were twenty feet long, and this was one of them. He was twice as long as a kayak.

What a prize, if they could take him before he took them.

Hal's head was not working well, and no wonder after his terrible experience. It was up to the 'kid brother' to do the thinking for both of them. Roger had an idea — but would it work?

As the bull came near, he struck it on its tender nose with his paddle. The bull sank. Soon it rose, bellowing, and again Roger gave it the sore nose treatment before it had a chance to breathe.

Again, down went the bull. But he *must* have air. So he was up again almost at once. Another resounding crack. And down went the breathless sea horse.

Hal saw what Roger was trying to do — make the animal go weak for lack of air — and he joined in.

Finally the great beast's eyes closed and he gave up struggling. Two boys had conquered him, simply by preventing him from filling his lungs.

Now they had to act fast. The bull might recover, and defeat them after all. They threw both lassos over his head and towed the unconscious monster to shore.

Many men had gathered to see the show. They knew the boys and liked them. They saw what was needed and had a truck with a drag behind. The drag, a sort of raft, was pushed under the walrus while still in the water — then they started the truck and pulled the drag and its ton-and-a-half load all the way to the airport.

The walrus did not recover until he was safely stowed into a skyvan, ready for the trip to Long Island.

17
Roger and the Killer

A voice outside the igloo called: 'Somebody wants to come in.'

'Who is it?' said Hal. He got no answer. Then he remembered — no Eskimo would give his name — that would offend the name-ghost.

If it was Zeb, Hal certainly did not want him to come in. But Zeb wouldn't say 'Somebody'. So it must be an Eskimo.

'Somebody may come in,' Hal said.

Olrik entered. He was amazed to see the brothers dressed in their Neoprene rubber diving suits. Each carried a scuba breathing tank on his back.

'What's up?' said Olrik. 'Going for a swim just for fun? Or business?'

'You might call it business,' Hal said. 'We got a telegram. Dad wants a killer whale.'

'A killer whale! Why, you poor dopes — you'll get murdered. We Eskimos know the killer whale. He's about the most dangerous visitor we have in these waters. Many of them have just arrived. Everybody is staying off the ice for fear of being gobbled up by a killer whale.'

'Perhaps they come so seldom that your people

have never really become acquainted with them. Have you ever seen one?'

'Can't say I have. But there are a lot of stories. Some of our own friends have been killed by those brutes.'

Hal said, 'No one can see very well under water. Perhaps what got them was a shark.'

'But surely you know the reputation of the killer whale,' said Olrik.

'Yes, it has a terrible reputation,' Hal replied. 'It is only about thirty feet long and can kill a whale a hundred feet long. It has twenty-four teeth as sharp as razors. It bites a whale on the corner of its mouth, makes it open its jaws and then it proceeds to eat the tongue. For some reason that makes the whale almost helpless. It begins to bleed to death. The killer goes on until it has filled its six-foot-long stomach and then other killers come in and do the rest.'

'Well then,' said Olrik, 'if you know it's so terrible why go down after it?'

'Because it happens to be one of man's best friends. People call it a whale but it isn't. It is a big dolphin. And dolphins never attack men. They seem to think that we are their cousins.'

'I'm no cousin of any killer,' said Olrik.

Hal went on, 'I wish I could introduce you to a killer whale.'

'You want to get me murdered?'

'Certainly not. But I know you'd be safe. I know he would like you.'

'You're right. He'd like me so well he'd eat me up.'

'Not a chance. In all the zoos where they have dolphins they are the best performers. They can do no end of tricks. They are very easy to teach. The elephant is a fine animal and has a great brain. But the brain of a killer whale is seven times as large as the brain of an elephant.'

'That doesn't mean anything,' said Olrik. 'A big brain that thinks of nothing but mischief is not as good as a small brain that behaves itself.'

'That is true, Olrik,' said Hal. 'But now if you will excuse us we're off to see if the big brain can also behave itself.'

'Well,' said Olrik, 'it's been nice knowing you. I suppose I'll never see you again, so here's goodbye.'

'Not a long goodbye,' said Hal, 'but just a short one. See you at lunch.'

It was now mid-summer, yet there was plenty of ice. They walked out on the drifting floes, jumping from one to another. If their jump was a bit short they would go into the sea long before they intended to. When they were far enough out to know that they were over deep water, they slid down into the sea.

The water was cold, but their rubber suits kept them as warm as toast.

They looked about with great care. It was not a killer whale that they were looking for just now, but a shark. The shark was no friend of man.

As bad luck would have it they glimpsed one which was coming their way. They shot up like two bolts of lightning and clambered up on to a floe.

Olrik, on the shore, was amused. 'They're running away from the killer whale already.'

He expected to see the snout of a killer whale rise above the surface. Instead he saw the jaws of a shark shoot out of the water, reach for the boys, sink again.

The floe that they were on was drifting with the current. Not until it had floated a quarter of a mile did the boys once more drop into the sea.

No shark was in sight, nor was a killer whale.

They could see a great object like a submarine coming their way. It had its huge mouth wide open. Hal guessed that it was a Greenland whale.

It was a whale with no teeth.

How can any animal get its food if it has no teeth?

There are two kinds of whales — those with teeth, and those without. The toothed whales include the beaked whale, the white whale, the goose-beaked whale, the sperm whale and others. On the other hand the whales without teeth are the humpback, the finback, the grey, the sei, the right and the blue. Largest of all is the blue whale, one hundred feet long, the largest animal in the world, equal in size to 150 oxen or twenty-five big elephants.

How do these monsters live? Simply by swimming along with their mouths open and taking in anything that gets in the way — the tiny living things called plankton, also crabs, lobsters, shrimps and what-not.

This might seem like small stuff for such a huge animal, but they succeed in putting away about a ton of food a day — and without taking one bite. What an easy way to live!

The Greenland whale, swimming along with eyes shut and mouth open, was as surprised as Roger was when the boy was scooped up by those great jaws.

He could not be chewed because there were no teeth. He could not be swallowed because the throat of the animal was too small. He was just stuck. His feet dangled out of one side of the mouth and his hands out of the other. And if there was any bellowing to be done, Roger did it. But if you try to howl inside a whale's mouth, you might as well save your breath. You cannot be heard.

The whale stopped. He was very much annoyed by this squirming thing in his mouth. He tried to get rid of it but it was stuck fast.

Hal sympathized with the whale, as well as with his brother. There was nothing he could do. He was unusually strong, and weighed more than his own father, but what chance did he have against this monster that weighed perhaps a hundred times as much?

He grabbed Roger's feet to pull him out. He could not move him one inch. He went to the other side and took hold of Roger's hands. These he pulled lustily but with no effect.

He looked around for help.

It came in the shape of a young killer whale, not more than fifteen feet long, who saw the two boys and came to the rescue. He thrust his head into the great mouth and closed his jaws on Roger. The sharp teeth were not too comfortable but they did not penetrate the heavy rubber suit. With a thrash of his tail the killer whale propelled himself backward and pulled Roger out of the jaws of death.

The Greenland whale made off with all speed because he was no friend of the killer whale.

The whale who was not a whale was apparently

reluctant to leave. He rubbed his head dog-fashion against Roger and then, in order not to have any favourites, he gave Hal the same treatment. When they rose to the surface he was with them.

Their faithful friend, Olrik, had a truck and drag waiting for them. The young killer whale was hauled on to the drag and the boys got into the truck. Away they went to the airport.

'We'll have to hurry,' Hal said. 'No whale or dolphin is any good until he is in the water. His lungs are in his chest. The weight of his body presses down so hard that he cannot get enough air into his lungs and will suffocate. He may be dead before we can get him into a skyvan. Those tanks we saw at the airport — could we have one put into the skyvan at once?'

'It's in already,' Olrik said. 'I knew you'd need it.

It's twenty feet long, about five feet longer than the animal. And it's full of water.'

'Bless you, Olrik. I don't know what I'd do without you,' said Hal gratefully.

The killer whale was still alive when it was put into the tank. It would never need to kill again. It would be fed as soon as it arrived at Long Island, and then it would be tanked to the zoo that had ordered it. There it would be happy, learning the various acts required of it more quickly than any other swimming animal because as the scientist Dr Lilly had said, 'Dolphins learn as fast as humans.'

18
His Tooth is Nine Feet Long

'Now we are asked to get a narwhal,' said Hal.

Roger's forehead wrinkled. He thought he knew animals pretty well but he had never heard of this one. 'What's a narwhal?'

'It's one of the most peculiar animals on the face of the earth. It's found only in the Arctic, so most people have never heard of it.'

'What is it — a whale?'

'No, it's not a whale.'

'A fish?'

'No, it's not a fish.'

'Well then, what is it?'

'It's a narwhal.'

'Don't beat about the bush. What the dickens is a narwhal?'

'Something like the unicorn.'

'All right then, what's a unicorn?'

'Something that isn't. It doesn't exist and it never did. But people two thousand years ago believed in it. It was supposed to be a kind of horse, but the odd thing about it was that it was thought to have a horn protruding many feet in front of the head. So it was called a unicorn — *uni* meaning one and *corn* from the Latin *cornu* meaning horn. The explorers found a horn of solid ivory, the very best. Only animals produce ivory, therefore they decided that this must come from a real unicorn. They told the world that they had proof that the beast called a unicorn really existed. Actually it was the tooth of a narwhal. It was nine feet long.'

Roger said, 'You can't tell me that any animal has a tooth nine feet long.'

'We'll see, when we get one. A very peculiar thing about the narwhal is that it has only two teeth. The one on the right side is just a small tooth, the one on the left is nine feet long — sometimes ten.'

Roger shook his head. 'I still don't believe that there's anything on earth like that. I've been in a lot of zoos and never saw one.'

'Most zoo men don't know anything about it. The New York Aquarium in Coney Island had a very small one. It was said to be the first narwhal that had ever been captured alive. It refused to eat fish. But it did like milk shakes. It gained twenty pounds in a week on milk shakes. That was in 1969. If it grew up it would be twenty feet long by this time. I have no idea whether it lived or not. But up here they come and go, sometimes a thousand of them at a time.'

'So perhaps we won't see one of them or we may see a thousand.'

'That's the way it goes,' said Hal. 'The Eskimos kill them for their meat, which is delicious. Olrik told me that the Eskimos once killed a thousand narwhals. They left the meat on an ice floe and a gale came along and swept it out to sea. The meat was lost to the bears.'

'Are the horns any good?'

'They are ground into powder and sold to the Chinese, who think they are wonderful medicine. And tourists who come to Greenland like to take home a foot or two of horn with a carving on it done by some talented Eskimo artist. A fine carving on pure ivory brings quite a lot of money.'

Olrik came to tell them, 'Now's your chance to get a narwhal. They haven't come in thousands as they sometimes do, but there are at least a hundred offshore.'

'A hundred is more than we need,' said Hal. 'Just one will do.'

'Well it won't be easy to get one. They swim like lightning. But if anybody can get one I know you can. I'm so sure of that that I'll have a truck and a drag ready when you come ashore with it.'

Hal and Roger went out in their two rented kayaks. Olrik was right — there were a hundred or more narwhals having a grand time leaping over each other, poking each other playfully with their horns, shooting down to the bottom to scratch up halibut. Those that were at rest stood upright in the water, their horns standing straight up above the surface so they looked like dozens of posts, all about nine feet high. Suddenly the posts would disappear and the water would boil with the antics of these lively animals. They treated the kayaks like new playthings. They bumped them into the air and they actually slid across the front deck and the rear deck but never touched the boy who occupied the hole in the middle.

Hal tried repeatedly to catch one with his lasso but it only slid on to the horn and was shaken off again.

Roger did better, without trying. A rollicking narwhal plunged his horn through the sealskin sides of the kayak so far that it came out of the other side. It barely missed Roger himself. It tore a hole big enough to let the water in, and the kayak with Roger inside it began to sink. Once locked into a kayak it is very difficult to escape. The narwhal also was trying to get out, but without success.

Hal brought his kayak up beside Roger's. 'Break loose,' he said, 'and scramble out of there fast.'

Roger was already up to his neck in water. Hal threw his lasso over the boy's head and hauled him out.

'Lie flat on the deck behind me,' he said.

Roger had never been noosed before but he was glad to be rescued from a watery grave. He grabbed the gunwhale of the sinking kayak and held on with all his strength. The narwhal had given up struggling to get free. Hal paddled toward shore and Roger never let go of the kayak and its horny passenger.

Olrik was ready with truck and drag. 'That's a new way to catch a narwhal,' he said.

Hal paid the kayak owner a little extra for repairs to his boat. A patch of sealskin over each hole would quickly restore the boat to its proper condition. The narwhal was transported to the airport.

The news travelled fast through the city of Thule and the paper the next morning praised Hal and especially Roger for doing what had never been done before in Greenland. It was easy to take a narwhal dead, but a fifteen-year-old boy had taken one alive.

'It's all nonsense,' said Roger. 'I didn't catch him. He caught himself.'

19
Monster with Ten Arms

'Somebody wants to tell you something very important.'

'That sounds like Olrik,' said Hal. 'If your name is Olrik, come in. If your name is Zeb, don't.'

Olrik came in. He said, 'Have you heard about the sea serpent?'

'No,' said Hal. 'The last time I heard about a sea serpent was when I was eight years old. My father told me there was no such thing.'

'Then it probably isn't a sea serpent. But it's Something very strange. The whole town is worried about it. Women are weeping because they have lost their children. Men are sharpening up their harpoons to kill the Something.'

'What is this Something like?'

'It's like a snake. It reaches up out of the water and grabs whatever it can find on a floe. It takes a seal, or a baby walrus, or a seagull. That wasn't so bad, but when this Something began to take down boys and girls and even grown-ups who had come to watch, everybody got excited and they want you to do something about it.'

'It must have powerful jaws', said Hal, 'to pull

men and women as well as children down into the
sea.'

'It has no jaws, no fangs, no mouth, no eyes. In
fact, it has no head. Where its head should be, it
has a hand. It's a very powerful hand and even when
it closes on a strong man he can't resist it. Down he
goes into the ocean.'

'A snake that has a hand where its head should
be,' said Hal. 'Sounds pretty fantastic.'

'Come and see for yourself,' said Olrik.

'We sure will. We can't tell much by looking at it
from a floe. We'll have to get on our diving suits and
go down. Perhaps it's something that a zoo would
like to have.'

The Eskimos on the ice floes watching this strange
Something were glad to see Hal and Roger. They
were astonished when they saw that the boys carried
no weapons, no harpoons, nothing but a coil of rope.

'Don't go down there,' someone shouted. 'You'll
get killed.'

'He may be right,' Hal said. 'No need for both of
us to go down. You stay here.'

Hal sank into the sea. Roger waited until his
brother was well out of sight, then he joined him.

What they saw was no serpent. It was more like
a lot of serpents. Hal counted them. There were ten.
And all of them sprouted from one body. Judging
by its size, Hal reckoned it must weigh a thousand
pounds. The most terrible thing about its appearance were its huge black eyes, almost a foot in diameter. It had terrific jaws, large enough to take in

Roger at one gulp. With its tentacles stretched out it must measure fifty feet from tip to tip.

Hal knew what it was. It was the giant cuttle, which has various other names such as giant squid, devilfish and cuttlefish.

It was quite at home in all oceans, including the Arctic, and was so strong that it could drag down a large boat. It was the world's largest invertebrate, that is, an animal without a backbone. It was carnivorous — nothing but meat would satisfy it. And here, before its nose, were two fine chunks of meat.

But it had evidently dined so well that it was not hungry. Instead it was startled and a little frightened by these two animals that did not seem to be afraid of it.

It waved its tentacles about, and it was easy to see that on each one there were four rows of cups, each cup full of sharp edges like knives. In fact that was why it was called a cuttle. Cuttle is a very ancient word meaning knife. When these suction cups were clamped on any prey the knives began their work and the victim was dead long before it reached the monster's jaws.

Every tentacle did look like a snake, but it ended not in a head but in a sort of hand which could firmly clutch and hold any living object.

Hal had learned that this peculiar beast had a shell — but the shell was not on the outside, but inside the body. Though inside, it protected the heart and other organs.

Disturbed by the boys, the peculiar beast spouted a cloud of ink into the water which entirely concealed

him from sight. That was why it had still another name — the pen-and-ink fish.

Hal feared that the cuttle behind the cloud of ink would now swim away. It would swim backwards, forcing itself along by jets of water from its siphons — a method copied by the makers of jet planes. Men had learned something very valuable from this remarkable Something.

Hal and Roger burst through the ink cloud, determined that this marvellous creature should not escape. The monster, preparing to swim, brought all its ten arms in close to the body. Hal slipped his lasso over the head and back over the body. Then he pulled it tight, imprisoning not only the body but the ten 'serpents'. Roger helped to adjust the loop and got for his pains a slash from a tentacle with its dozens of knives. The result was that his Neoprene suit was badly cut and would need a lot of repairs before it could be made waterproof again.

His skin had been badly gouged and the blood

that came from the wounds made another cloud, this time of red, beside the black cloud of the cuttle's ink.

The boys then carried the end of the heavy rope up to a floe, where it was seized by a dozen men. Inch by inch the prize exhibit was drawn out of the water and began its journey to the airport.

20
Living under Ice

They walked the streets of Thule — Hal, Roger and Olrik.

'Quite a town,' said Hal.

'Sixteen streets,' said Olrik, 'and a radar tower fifty feet higher than the Empire State Building.'

'All I see is shops, shops, shops,' said Hal. 'Where are the people who live here?'

'The big bosses live in these houses. The working men live under the ice.'

Hal stopped and stared at Olrik. 'You don't mean that.'

'Of course I do. Haven't you been down under?'

'No. I've had all I can handle on top.'

'Come with me,' said Olrik. 'I'll show you the under-ice city.'

Outside Thule they reached a hole in the ground. A stairway took them down to the strangest town they had ever seen.

It consisted of immense metal tubes twenty-six feet in diameter. These tubes were the streets of the town. The floor was made of planks. Along the side of the tube were cabins where the working men lived.

'But why don't they build the cabins up on top?' said Hal.

'Because they would soon be buried in snow. Once they were up above, and the snow completely covered them. So they went below where the snow can't get at them.'

There was not a glimpse of daylight but there were plenty of electric lights. 'It's like being in a submarine,' Roger said.

But this was much larger than any submarine ever built. There were several dining-rooms. There was a library. There was a game room with table tennis. There was a radio room. There was a gymnasium, and a theatre where, Olrik said, you could see the latest American films even before they were shown in America.

'How far down are we?' Hal asked.

'Thirty-six feet below the surface,' said Olrik, 'and getting deeper every time we have a snowstorm.'

'Doesn't the snow on top keep it very cold down here?'

'On the contrary, snow keeps it warm. It's a very good insulator.'

Men who happened to be off duty were having a good time — looking at films, playing games, reading, singing, talking politics, protected from any bad weather that might happen to be outside.

The boys came out into a snowstorm. A chill wind was blowing. They had to admit it was much better under the ice.

A few days later Olrik took them to another under-ice city. It was called Camp Century and it was even larger and better than the first. Main Street was a quarter of a mile long. It was covered by iron sheets above which was snow many feet deep. When rain came the snow turned to ice.

'Those iron sheets will be removed after a time,' said Olrik.

'Doesn't the snow fall in?' said Hal.

'No,' said Olrik. 'After the snow becomes hard it is able to support itself.'

Main Street was very busy. It was so high and wide that tractors and trucks that Olrik called weasels were able to pass through without difficulty. There were fourteen cross streets. They were lined with cabins made of plastic.

'We think plastic will be used a lot in the ice-sheet stations of the future,' Olrik said. 'It makes good, tight little houses.'

In the centre of the town there was a nuclear power plant to provide all the electricity needed in the little city.

'Sometimes it is too warm,' said Olrik.

'Do you get cold air from above?' Hal asked.

'No, from below.'

'How could you do that?'

'Holes have been bored forty feet down into the ice and fans bring up the cold air.'

They visited the quarters of the officers. They were large, lovely rooms with leather-covered armchairs, mahogany chests, decorated lamps, thick carpets and everything else that an officer could desire.

This modern town under the ice was designed for one hundred and fifty men, but Olrik said it would soon be enlarged to accommodate a thousand.

Some of the rooms that Hal and his companions

visited were twenty-four feet wide and two hundred feet long. One of these was a laboratory in which experiments were being made to improve still further this unique city under the ice.

21
Hal Rides an Iceberg

'Would you like to go to the iceberg coast?' Olrik said one morning.

Hal was surprised. 'You mean Greenland's east coast? That's eight hundred miles away. By dog team it would take twenty-five days to get there.'

'I see you have been reading up on it,' said Olrik. 'You're a pretty thoroughgoing chap. You always look before you leap.'

'Cut the compliments,' Hal said. 'All I know is that we have no chance of getting to the east coast. It must be wonderful. Most of the world's icebergs are born there. But we can't afford to spend twenty-five days to get there and twenty-five days back.'

'Well then,' said Olrik, 'how about half a day to get there and half a day back?'

'Dream on,' laughed Hal. 'You can only do that by plane. And we have no plane.'

'Yes you have, if you want it. You know I work at the airport part time. A fellow I know is going to fly over to inspect a mining operation. I asked him if he could take you along. He would be glad to have your company. It's lonesome flying alone. The young fellow is called Pete. He'll be leaving at eight this morning. It's nearly that now. Get on some very warm clothing because it's mighty cold over there.'

They dressed warmly and accompanied Olrik to the airport, where they met Pete. He shook hands with them.

'Glad to have you along,' he said. 'Hop in.'

They climbed aboard. Something above them began to whirr.

'So you fly a helicopter,' said Hal.

'I fly almost anything,' said Pete, 'but a helicopter is best on this trip because landing on the cliffs of the east coast is sometimes pretty difficult.'

'I understand,' said Hal. 'The helicopter lets you down easy. You don't need a runway.'

'That's right,' said Pete. 'It's pretty wild over there. Nothing but cliffs and glaciers. No runways. No trees, no grass, nothing but ice and snow and precipices. It's a bad place to live, a good place to die.'

Now they were crossing the great Greenland ice cap. 'They say', Hal remarked, 'that this ice cap is millions of years old. The oldest part of it, of course, is at the bottom. What would happen if the whole ice cap melted some day during a warm spell along with the one at the South Pole and became just a part of the sea?'

Pete answered, 'If they melted, it would raise the level of the sea 245 feet.'

'Think of that!' said Hal. 'All the cities along the coast from New York to Buenos Aires would be drowned.'

Roger said, 'Has anybody ever bored down through the ice cap to the bottom?'

'No, they bored a hole fifty feet deep and found that the snow there had been laid down in 1879.'

'Why don't they bore deeper?'

'Because the ice cap is twisting like a snake. If you should bore a straight hole today it would be a crooked hole tomorrow. It would be so twisted that you couldn't possibly get to the bottom of it. Nobody can imagine how this ice cap moves about. There are a few stations on the ice sheet but you don't know where to find them. They wander here and there. The moving ice carried one station 550 feet in a year. Another station moved half a mile south. The ice cap is alive and kicking. It has a mind of its own.'

Roger looked off to the north-east. 'Do those black clouds mean it's going to snow or rain?'

'Those are not clouds,' said Pete. 'They are mountains. They're called the Watkin Mountains. They are 12,200 feet high. And the mine I am going to see is bored right into the side of one of them. I'll take you to the iceberg area and leave you there while I go on to the mine. I'll be there two or three days, then come back and pick you up.'

'That's all right with us,' said Hal. 'We have a tent and our sleeping bags, and provisions.'

As they neared the east coast they could see the ocean covered with icebergs. Hal remembered how a mighty iceberg such as these had sunk the great ship *Titanic* in 1912. It was the largest ship in the world and it was making its first voyage. Its captain believed in speed, he couldn't wait for anything, because he wanted to break the trans-Atlantic record. The sea was very calm and the night was clear and cold. The captain knew there were icebergs ahead but he depended upon a sharp lookout rather than reducing speed.

The lookout wasn't sharp enough. Faster than any ship afloat at that time, the *Titanic* ploughed head-on into an iceberg which split the ship open as if it had been a walnut. Water rushed in and the ship began to sink. Down to their death went 1,500 passengers.

Perhaps the captain had thought that his mighty ship could plough right through any iceberg. He was sadly mistaken. The berg was just chipped a little, while the ironbound ship became in one moment a pile of junk.

The captain was severely criticized for his carelessness but that did not bring 1,500 people back to life.

Another careless fellow was the captain of the ship *Californian*, which was only ten miles away but did not respond to the distress signal and simply went on its way without offering any help to the sinking ship and people.

Looking down from the helicopter the boys could see rivers on their way to the ocean. These were not rivers of water but rivers of ice.

'Those glaciers are very deep,' Pete said. 'Some of them almost a thousand feet from top to bottom. One is seven hundred miles long — the longest in the world. Of course being solid ice, they move very slowly, about a hundred feet in a year. But they finally get to the edge of the cliff overlooking the sea. They don't stop there. Pushed from behind, the glacier keeps going right on into the air. It may ooze

126

out anywhere from a hundred to five hundred feet. But it has nothing to hold it up, so finally, with a terrific crash, it falls three hundred feet to the sea. And that means a new iceberg.'

Roger was excited. 'I want to see that.'

'You'll see it. And you'll hear it — the cracking and groaning and thundering of the glacier and the terrible crash when it falls into the water throwing up fountains in every direction.'

'And that's what they call calving,' said Hal.

'Yes,' said Pete. 'It's a strange way to describe it, but it means that just as a cow gives birth to a calf so the glacier gives birth to an iceberg. I must say an iceberg is a mighty big calf.'

Pete couldn't land his helicopter where he wanted to. The 100-mile-an-hour wind so common on this coast blew the helicopter out over the sea and a wind current carried it down almost to the water. Pete worked hard to get his machine up again into the air. He circled a couple of icebergs, always in danger of striking one, and finally got the flying machine up above the cliff. There he brought it to a wobbly landing.

Hal and Roger piled out with their tent, sleeping bags and provisions.

'Good luck,' cried Pete, as he turned his plane to the north and took off for the mine.

Roger shivered. 'What makes it so awfully cold here? It's much colder than it was on the other coast and that was cold enough.'

Hal replied, 'There's no north-flowing current here as there was on the other coast to warm it up a little bit. On this side there's nothing but cold current coming from the north.'

Roger drew his parka around over his face. His breath made his face damp. He pulled his parka away in order to see. At once the moisture on his skin froze and his face was encased in ice. Even his eyelids were frozen together. He could dimly see through his lashes.

'Why did that happen?' he wanted to know.

'It's a lot colder here than on the ice cap,' said Hal.

'I'll run around and get warm,' Roger said.

'You'd better not. You will sweat and the sweat will turn to ice. Then you'll be covered from top to toe with ice.'

Crash, crash, crash. More and more icebergs where there were plenty already.

'What good are icebergs anyhow?' Roger said. 'Why don't the engineers find a way to prevent them?'

'They have tried,' said Hal. 'They have shot them with cannon. They have bombed them. They've drilled and blasted them. They have painted them black to make them melt more quickly. All these measures have failed.'

'But surely they must melt after a while.'

'Yes, after a while. But it's a good long while. An iceberg will last more than a year. Very large icebergs take much longer to melt. Some bergs are seven hundred feet high and weigh eight million tons. They may last for years. Storms make them crash into each other and chip off ice. But not enough is chipped off to have any great effect.'

They put up the tent and anchored it firmly so that the wind would not blow it away. Then Hal said, 'Let's take a walk.'

'Where?'

'Out on this glacier.'

'But the glacier will take us out and drop us into the sea.'

'I think we can get off in time,' said Hal. 'It only moves very slowly.'

So they walked on the groaning, grinding glacier, which was not as smooth as they expected. It had many furrows and ridges and holes. Roger got tired and went back to the tent. He crawled into his sleeping bag to warm up. He took a nap — then was roused by a scream louder than the crashing of icebergs.

He jumped out to see what was going on. He saw his brother falling through space. Hal had gone out too far on the glacier as it reached out over the sea, and when it broke off he went down with it. There, far below, was Hal floating away on an iceberg.

What could Roger do? Even if he could get down the 300-foot cliff he could do nothing. Hal's berg was already too far away.

'If only I had a boat,' Roger thought.

There must be someone, somewhere, living on top of this cliff. Roger ran north through deep snow. He did just what Hal had warned him against. He began to sweat, and the sweat turned to ice. Now he was an ice man and could hardly move his joints. There was no sign of a house or hut or igloo. No one was fool enough to live here.

He turned about and ran south. All he

accomplished was to make more sweat which turned into more ice on his body.

He looked out to sea, hoping he could signal a ship. There was no ship to be seen. No ship was likely to sail into this ocean of icebergs.

He must do something about this coat of ice he was wearing. It was getting more and more difficult to move.

He went into the tent and lit the little camp stove. Then he took off all of his clothes and stood as stiff as a statue while his icy armour began to melt. When it had turned to water and run off him he dried himself with a towel and dressed. Then he went out and looked but he could not see Hal now. His iceberg had floated too far away.

He felt like crying but he was too old to cry. He was a big boy and a big boy should be able to do something. But he was helpless. He went back inside and got into his sleeping bag.

He could not sleep. Every time he was about to drift off he thought someone had left him all alone at the North Pole.

'Never mind,' he told himself. 'When Hal gets beyond the iceberg area some ship will come along and rescue him.'

If only Pete would come back now rather than wait two or three days. Pete would know what to do. He could fly south and perhaps he would find Hal.

But it was four sleeps before Pete came back.

'Hal is way off somewhere floating on an iceberg. He hasn't had any food for four days and he must be just about dead.'

131

'Let's go find him,' said Pete.

They flew away in the direction that Hal's iceberg had floated. They did not find the floating boy. They searched among all the icebergs but caught no sight of him.

Roger, with sinking heart, said, 'Let's go outside the iceberg area.'

They went outside and within an hour they came upon a small fishing vessel and there was Hal upon its deck as neat and fat and chipper as ever.

The helicopter came near and hovered above the deck. A rope ladder was lowered and Hal climbed to the helicopter. He waved his thanks to the captain of the fishing boat.

Roger's first question was, 'Did you get anything to eat?'

'I was three days without anything to chew but the iceberg,' Hal said. 'Then we floated outside the ice pack and this fishing boat took me in and fed me.'

Roger was happy — and angry.

'You gave me the heebie-jeebies,' he said.

Hal smiled, 'Sorry, my boy, that you had to eat alone while I starved on an iceberg.'

Roger was too glad to get his brother back to do any more grouching.

They flew back to the cliff and struck camp, climbed aboard the helicopter again, and in four hours were in their own igloo, where Nanook gave them a warm and sloppy reception, standing up on his hind feet and licking their faces as if they had been away for a year instead of only four days.

22
Hurricane

'We've got to get a polar bear to send home,' said Hal.

'We already have one,' said Roger. 'Nanook.'

Hal said, 'We'd hate to part with Nanook. He's a member of our family. I mean this little family that we have in our igloo. Nanook and you and myself. And he's so fond of us I doubt he'd be happy without us.'

'Where would we go to get another? Up on the ice cap?'

'We might go miles without finding one,' said Hal. 'I think the best place to get one is Hudson Bay. They say there are plenty of them in a town called Churchill.'

Roger laughed. 'We go to town to find a polar bear?'

'I know it seems strange — but that's just where you would find a lot of them. Right in town on the main street.'

'You're kidding. Where did you get that crazy idea?'

'From an article in the *Smithsonian*. That's the official magazine of the Smithsonian Institution in

Washington. It's the national museum of the United States. I think we can believe anything they say.'

'But how do we get there?'

'A brig is sailing for Churchill tomorrow. We'll be on it. Don't expect any luxuries. It's no ocean liner. Usually a brig just carries sails. But this one has both sails and engine. I think it will get us there without trouble.'

It wasn't Hal's fault that he was making a wrong guess. He couldn't foresee the coming hurricane.

Two hours after they boarded the little vessel, the sky exploded. A terrific wind had come up. It was so violent that it threatened to carry away the sails, so they had to be brought down. The wind shrieked and wailed. A violent ice storm attacked the little vessel.

There was a grinding and thrashing sound as millions of tons of ice under the force of the gale beat upon the small ship. Ice floes ten or twenty feet thick screeched and roared as they attacked the brig.

No boiler factory could produce such a racket. The Arctic Ocean has been called the silent sea, but there was no silence aboard the *Happy Waters*. Hal and Roger, side by side as they clung to a mast in order to avoid being blown away, could not hear each other speak.

They wanted to go down below and get into their bunks, but then they would miss the show. It wasn't every day that you could see a hurricane in action. Everybody else was below except the captain.

They were ploughing through Melville Bay, which has the reputation of being the most dangerous in the Arctic. It was full of icebergs. They did not soar seven hundred feet high like those on the east coast. But even icebergs twice as tall as the ship presented a great danger. The brig was strongly built but the best hull can't stand a million tons of ice leaning against it.

Since only one-eighth of an iceberg shows above the surface, the seven-eighths below the surface is very likely to cause trouble. Time and time again the brig was nearly upset by the part of an iceberg reaching out below her keel. Once she tipped so far to starboard that all the passengers below fell out of their bunks. Sometimes the brig stuck fast and only the screaming wind was strong enough to move it onward.

The gale was roaring like a lion. The captain tried to bring his ship around into the lee of an iceberg where it would get less wind. He had no sooner done this than the iceberg that sheltered the brig was pushed into another berg and the ship was squeezed between them. Since both bergs slanted, the ship was hoisted up in the air until she was raised ten feet above the raging sea.

There she was, no longer tipping and teetering, but so still that the passengers put their heads up to see if the boat was in some harbour. They were astonished to see their craft stuck up in the air above the dashing waves. Now for a little time at least the ship was still and they had a chance to get over their seasickness.

But this was not getting them to Churchill. And the captain was distressed for fear the pressure on both sides would break the hull. Then everything and everybody would go down to the bottom, where there was perfect peace and death. For twelve hours the ship remained suspended in the air.

The passengers complained about the bothersome bergs.

Hal told them, 'There's only one nice thing about bergs. That drink you are swallowing wouldn't be half as good without icebergs.'

'You're off your head,' said one gruff fellow. 'What do icebergs have to do with a drink?'

'The ice in it is the very best. Greenland exports iceberg ice all over the world. Every summer at least ten Greenland icebergs are cut into small chunks and shipped abroad. They have a trade name, "Greenland Iceberg Rocks".'

The passengers grinned and rattled the 'Rocks' in their glasses. For the moment they were amused, but soon became grouchy again.

One complained to the captain. 'Why don't you do something?' he asked angrily.

'If you tell me what to do,' said the captain, 'I'll do it.'

'Well,' said the man, 'it's perfectly simple. Just push one of the bergs away and the ship will drop into the water.'

The captain smiled. 'Suppose *you* push it away. I'm sure it doesn't weigh more than a million tons.'

Finally the hurricane passed and the powerful wind that had held the two bergs in place relaxed. The ship slid into the sea, and the voyage continued. Passing through Hudson Strait, the brig crossed Hudson Bay to the small town called Churchill.

23
City of Polar Bears

Hal and Roger walked into a small hotel on the Churchill waterfront and asked the man at the desk for a room.

'Yes, I have one room left. Number eight on the ground floor. You'll find it easily. The door is open.'

They found the open door and walked into their room. But the room was already occupied. Hal stopped and stared. He could hardly believe what he saw.

'I'll be hornswoggled,' he said.

Sitting on a low stool was a polar bear.

'Let's get out of here — fast,' said Roger.

'Wait a minute,' Hal said. The bear did not even look at them. He seemed to be very much at home. He did not move.

The boys went back to the office. 'There's a bear in our room,' said Hal.

'Don't let that bother you,' said the proprietor.

'Why shouldn't it bother us?' Hal demanded.

'Just let him be. Sooner or later he'll walk away.'

'Is it a tame bear?'

'Far from it. He's as wild as they come. He could kill you with one swat if he didn't like you. In

Churchill we are very careful not to annoy our bears.'

'You mean that the bears come first?'

'Always. You see, we have more bears than people. The population of Churchill consists of sixteen hundred people and two or three thousand bears. But not all the year long. Sometimes no bears at all — sometimes thousands. I can promise that if you stay a few months you will find no bears in Churchill.'

'A few months!' exclaimed Hal. 'We can't stay here more than a few days.'

'Then you may as well prepare to enjoy our bears. We like them. Sure, they kill a few of us every year.

138

But most of them are all right if you just leave them alone. If you get a polar bear cross he's far more dangerous than a grizzly. So, go easy.'

They went back and peeked into their room. The bear had gone.

They flopped down on the beds to rest a while after the hard trip on the brig.

Then they went out to see the town. In the main street there were more bears than people. Why did the police allow this?

'It's too small a town to have a police force,' said Hal. 'But there's a Mountie.'

'What's a Mountie?' asked Roger.

'A member of the Royal Canadian Mounted Police,' said Hal.

The man who was called a Mountie because he was mounted on a horse, leaned down when Hal spoke to him.

Hal asked him, 'What do you do when one of these bears makes trouble? Do you shoot it?'

'Never, unless we have to,' said the Mountie. 'There's a law that protects the bears. There are only about twelve thousand of them still left in Canada. We don't want them to disappear entirely. If you kill one you go to jail — unless the bear has already killed you.'

'So your main job', said Hal, 'is to protect the bears, not the people.'

'Of course we protect the people. But there's no danger that they will disappear from the earth. So our main concern is to look out for the welfare of the bears. There's a Bear Patrol truck that keeps moving all day and all night around Churchill to see that the bears don't hurt people and the people don't hurt the bears.'

'One more question, officer. We represent an agency to provide wild animals to zoos. Would there be any objection to our taking one of your bears for a zoo?'

'Of course not. It would get better care in a zoo than it does in the wilderness. Just how you are going to manage it I can't imagine. But apparently you are bright fellows and you will find a way.'

The boys continued their walk. They were hungry, having had very little to eat on the brig. They found a small restaurant and went in. Of course there was a bear in the restaurant and everybody seemed to think this was quite proper. Bears had the right of way. A waiter served the bear a chunk of meat and demanded no payment.

The bear ate, and then, as if wishing to entertain the diners, he stood up on his hind feet. He was so tall that his head bumped the ceiling. This did not please him, and he growled. He came down on all four feet and walked out, shaking his head. Why couldn't people make their ceilings high enough so a bear could stand up? He didn't think much of people.

After lunch the boys took to the street again. They saw a bear at a window. He was not looking in the window. He was inside, looking out. This surprised the boys, but no one else looked twice. On one door they saw a sign, 'Club Members Only'. A bear tried to push his way in. A guard just inside yelled, 'You're not a member. Get out of here.' The bear walked away.

It happened to be Sunday and a church service was going on. A bear walked in. He proceeded solemnly up the aisle to the altar. The boys, looking in, saw one man who knew how to get rid of a bear. The organist produced such a terrific burst of music that the bear stopped in his tracks, trying to decide whether to eat the organist or escape from this terrible noise. The organist didn't look too tasty, so the visitor turned about and left.

Some people used firecrackers to frighten away a bear that became too inquisitive. One bear, terrified by the explosion within a few inches of his nose, took refuge in a bus. The boys saw their big chance. They closed the door of the bus. There were no people inside.

There was a driver in front protected by a heavy glass partition between himself and the rest of the bus. Hal spoke to him.

'Do you own this bus?'

'I do.'

'Have you ever been to Long Island, just outside New York?'

'I used to live in New York.'

'We want this bear for a zoo. The Mountie says we can have it. We'll pay you a hundred dollars if you'll take this bear to Long Island and deliver it to the Hunt Wild Animal Farm. If you don't know where it is, anybody there can tell you.'

'Make it two hundred and I'll do it,' said the bus owner. 'In advance.'

'Two hundred it is, but not in advance. How do we know you will really go through with it? I'll wire my father, John Hunt, who owns the farm, to pay you two hundred dollars upon arrival.'

'That's fair enough,' said the bus owner, and he lost no time in getting under way.

Hal sent this telegram to his father:

ONE THOUSAND-POUND POLAR BEAR COMING TO YOU BY BUS. UPON ARRIVAL PLEASE PAY DRIVER TWO HUNDRED DOLLARS PLUS FIFTY DOLLAR TIP IF THE BEAR IS ALIVE AND IN GOOD CONDITION.

They spent the night in the small hotel and then flew back to Greenland, having no desire for another battle with the icebergs of Melville Bay.

They embraced their own Nanook, and were thankful that it was not this dear friend that they were forced to part with.

'We'll stick by you,' Hal said, 'as long as you want to stick by us.'

24
Off to Alaska

'Why are you leaving Greenland?' Olrik complained. 'Don't you like it here?'

'Of course we like it,' Hal said. 'But we have done about all we can here. We have taken many animals and they have all been shipped home. Dad told us before we started this trip to go on to Alaska when we were finished here.'

'What could you expect to find in Alaska that we don't have in Greenland?'

'Well the Arctic moose, for example, the largest moose in the world. And the fighting fur seal, the sea lion, the sea otter and some kinds of whales that don't come into these waters. And the blue bear, the black bear, the grizzly. And the magnificent bighorn sheep. And, most important of all, the giant Kodiak bear, the greatest bear on earth.'

'That sounds wonderful,' Olrik admitted. 'But we sure will miss you.'

'We'll miss you a lot,' said Hal. 'You have been our best friend in Greenland. You lent us your fine dog team. You went with us on the ice cap and did everything in your power to help us. When we caught the walrus and the killer whale and the narwhal and the giant cuttle, you were right there on the shore with a truck and drag ready to take them to the airport. We would have had a hard time getting along without you.'

'Shucks,' said Olrik. 'I just enjoyed tagging along.'

'Will you tag along with us now? There's something in Thule I want to show you.'

In the town Hal stopped before a brand new house. Hal had hired workmen to build it and they had done a good job. It wouldn't be called a house in New York, but it was a house, and a good house, compared with an igloo or tent.

The walls were made of rocks fitted together and any cracks between them were filled with mud. The mud had frozen and would stay frozen in this land so close to the North Pole, where the temperature almost never rose above the freezing point. The flat roof was a criss-cross of bones from the skeletons of whales, covered by sod six inches thick. In the sod wildflowers were already blooming.

'A very good house,' said Olrik. 'Whose is it?'

'It's yours, you numskull — for you and your family.'

'I can't believe it,' said Olrik. 'My folks will love it. Every year we've had to rebuild our igloo. A solid rock house with a whalebone roof will never have to be rebuilt. Of course we'll pay for it — a little each year until it's all paid for.'

'Nonsense,' said Hal. 'You have already more than paid for it by all the things you have done for us.'

Hal and Roger went to see Aram, who had flown

them to the North Pole. Aram was still on crutches, and would perhaps stay on crutches for the rest of his life. He refused payment for the North Pole trip. His father would not take anything. His mother said, 'The spirits of all our ancestors fill this room. So long as we do good deeds they will not harm us. What we have done for you is very little and you will please forget it.'

Hal respected the old woman's fear of the spirits and left no money. He went to the doctor at the air base. He ordered and paid for a peg leg for Aram so that this brave young man would not have to go all the rest of his days on crutches.

Special attention had to be paid to Nanook. They were determined that he should be with them in Alaska. There was a regular air service to Alaska by cargo plane, but Hal had difficulty in convincing the authorities that a 1,000-pound polar bear should be considered as cargo.

'You say he is tame,' said the pilot. 'But perhaps he is just tame while you are around. He has never been in a plane before. I'm not going to make a flight to Alaska with a possible killer behind my back. I'll take him only on one condition — that you two go along with him in the cargo compartment.'

'We were planning to go in a comfortable passenger plane,' said Hal. 'We wouldn't enjoy very much going along with the boxes and bales in the cargo room. But if we have to we will do it.'

'Where do you want to be landed — at Fairbanks, or Anchorage?' said the pilot.

'No,' said Hal. 'Those are too far south. We want to set up our camp at Point Barrow first.'

'But that's the wildest part of Alaska. Point Barrow extends into the Arctic Ocean. It's only thirteen hundred miles from the North Pole. It's the most northern part of Alaska — the most northern part of the entire United States.'

'Just what we want,' said Hal. 'Our job there is to find Arctic sea animals. What better place to find them than the Arctic Ocean side of Alaska? Is there an airfield at Point Barrow?'

'Yes, we go there almost every day. Flying over the top of the world, it takes only five hours.'

'You mean you go over the North Pole?'

'Very close to it. Just a little to the left. It's the shortest way. We land at Point Barrow — then we go on south to the cities. You ought to go to Anchorage. It's on the southern edge and not as cold as everywhere else. It's a fine city. You'd like it.'

'I'm sure we would,' said Hal. 'But this is not a pleasure trip. For one thing, we want to go to the Brooks Range near Point Barrow.'

'The Brooks Range! Why, those mountains are eight thousand feet high. You'll freeze to death.'

'Yes,' said Hal, 'sometimes nine thousand. But if the animals can stand it, we can.'

Nanook did not show the least fear in this strange house in the sky so long as the boys were with him. It was a thrill to know that they were passing so near the very top of the world. After only five hours they came down on the airfield at Point Barrow.

The two boys and Nanook walked down to the little village of Barrow. Here they got food, rested overnight in a little lodging house, and set out early in search of anything they could find.

25
The Well-Dressed Sea Otter

The boys and Nanook stood on the beach. Behind them was Barrow village. Before them was the Arctic Ocean.

Not far out was a dark lump.

'What can that be?' Roger wondered.

The dark lump put up a long neck and a head that carried a pair of very bright eyes and long whiskers.

'It's a sea otter,' exclaimed Hal. 'Look at the size of it. It's twice as big as the otters we've seen down south. I'd say it's about seven feet long. That's the first animal we're going to get in Alaska.'

Nanook was interested. He was growling softly. Did he think that this was going to be his dinner?

'What's so great about a sea otter?' Roger asked.

'One thing is that it loves fun more than almost any other animal. Life is just one round of games for the sea otter. Then it has the finest and most expensive of the world's furs. It's coming closer. See how well dressed it is.'

The otter's coat was brown with a big orange spot like a headlight under the neck, and beautiful glints of gold and silver on its sides.

Hal said, 'Women used to pay 2,500 dollars for one skin, and it took several skins to make a coat.'

'You say "used to",' said Roger. 'Don't they still?'

'No more,' said Hal, 'unless they want to go to prison. So many used to be killed that the sea otters almost disappeared altogether. So a law was passed to put a stop to the killing, and now there are millions of sea otters here and in the Pribilof Islands near Alaska.'

The otter was going through all sorts of acrobatics. It was having a very good time. It leaped up four or five feet, then turned and dived straight down. It came up again with a rock oyster held in one flipper that was bent like a hand. The other flipper held two stones.

The animal lay on its back and placed one stone on its chest. It put the oyster on that stone. Then it brought the other stone down with its full strength and broke the shell into fragments. Then it ate the oyster.

Roger stared. 'I never saw anything like that in my life. Did somebody train it to do that?'

'No,' said Hal. 'All the otters do it. It gives you some idea of their intelligence.'

'Is the otter like a fish? Can it stay down under water if it wants to?'

Hal said, 'It's just like you. It has to come up for air. The only difference is that it does much better than you or I could. Without a scuba we could stay down no more than three minutes. The otter can remain under water for ten minutes.'

'In the winter, when the water is frozen over, what does it do?'

'It comes out on land before the water freezes. It's too smart to stay under the ice and be drowned. It may waddle across country to some lake that has no ice over it because there is a hot spring at the bottom. Or it may decide to stay home.'

'What do you mean, home?'

'Its home may be right here among these bushes. It digs a tunnel, about thirty feet long, and lines it with leaves, grass, and moss so that it will be comfortable.'

'Then you can trap it by closing the front door.'

'No, there's a back door also, deep in the bushes.'

'By jiminy,' said Roger, 'it thinks of everything. Has anybody been able to tame it?'

'Yes,' said Hal, 'I have read that in India and China it is trained to catch fish for its master, or drive the fish into the net. If it likes you it can become very affectionate. But you have to keep away from those sharp teeth. If you annoy it it may give you a very bad bite. But you would have no trouble. All animals seem to like you.'

Now the otter was afloat on its back, sound asleep.

'Look,' said Roger. 'Something is crawling up on its chest.'

'It's a baby otter,' said Hal. 'The big one must be its mother.'

The mother otter woke and nursed her young one. She cleaned the pup with her teeth and her tongue. Just for the fun of it she tossed the pup into the air and caught him again on her chest. The little one squealed for joy.

The mother had several ways of speaking. She could squeal, she could bark, she could growl.

A shark was prowling about. The mother otter tucked her young one under her arm and dived. When she came up she hugged the shore and put her baby up on the beach out of reach of the shark.

Roger began talking to the mother in the quiet way he always used when speaking to animals. The intelligent animal decided she was safer on the shore with these humans and a bear rather than in the water at the mercy of a hungry shark.

She joined her pup on the beach.

Hal said, 'Take the pup in your arms, Roger. Then we'll walk slowly toward the airport. I'm sure the mother will follow wherever we take her pup.'

And so it was that the best dressed of all the mammals was the first to be captured by the take-'em-alive men in Alaska.

Here, as in Greenland, there were cargo planes available, and one was made the home of the mother and youngster, to be joined by other animals before the flight to Long Island.

26
Battle of the Giants

Why is everything so large in Alaska? Alaska itself is the giant of the fifty American states. Texas is an enormous state — but Alaska is twice as large as Texas. It would take three Californias to make an Alaska. Mount McKinley is North America's highest mountain at 20,320 feet. Alaska actually has sixteen mountains higher than any in the lower forty-eight states!

The world's biggest moose, the world's biggest bear, the world's biggest animals of many kinds are all in Alaska.

And on this particular morning the boys set out to find a sea lion fourteen feet long, twice the length of the seven-foot sea lion of the California coast. Alaska's fur seal is the biggest and strongest of its kind.

Hal and Roger were out early, carrying — not a gun — but a net and a lasso. They arrived at the beach just in time to see the fight. A big sea-lion bull was tackling a giant fur seal.

'Why do they call it a sea lion?' Roger asked.

Hal said, 'The scientist who discovered it, Steller by name, called it the lion of the sea because it

151

looked so much like the African lion with its huge neck, massive shoulders and golden eyes. Also, it was as big as a full-grown lion. The one you see right there probably weighs a ton. The sea lion is said to be smarter than a lion — and it's a lot more intelligent than the average seal. The circus that wants an animal to do tricks chooses a sea lion because it can be trained very easily. Even the young one is born smart. It doesn't start blind like so many animals, but has its eyes wide open, can swim without learning how, and weighs a hundred pounds before it is two months old. You might say it is grown up when it is born. It starts out with excellent vision and good hearing. It can dive to more than a thousand feet — and a big adult can't do any better.'

The fur seal sprang out of the water like a dolphin, his whiskers waving in the breeze, and came down with a mighty thump upon the back of the sea lion.

Roger laughed. 'Makes me think of two boys playing leap frog,' he said.

'Yes,' said Hal, 'but these two fellows are not playing games. They'd just like to kill each other, that's all.'

The lion twisted out from under his enemy and gave the fur seal a terrific blow on the head with his powerful flipper, which was almost as strong as iron.

Then it was whiskers against whiskers. Each got the other's whiskers between his teeth and pulled. The result was a terrific roar of pain on both sides.

Pulling loose, the sea lion grabbed the fur seal's head and ducked it down under the water. There he held it tightly so that his enemy should die for lack of air.

The fur seal wrapped his long, strong hind flippers around the lion's head and pulled it down under.

'Now they'll both die,' exclaimed Roger.

But the fur seal's wives came to the rescue. The boys hadn't noticed them before. Hal made a quick count. 'There are thirty of them.'

'And all of them are wives of this one bull?'

'That's right. Sometimes a bull has as many as fifty wives.'

With a great deal of squeaking the wives swam under the two males and hoisted their heads into the air.

The wives got small thanks from their bull. Instead, he roared at them as if he were saying, 'Get out of the way. This is no business for females.'

Hal said, 'He reminds me of some men who don't appreciate what their wives do for them.'

Now there was a furious struggle between the lion and the bull. At one moment it looked as if the fur bull would slaughter the lion. All eight flippers of the two beasts were going like windmills. One thinks of a flipper as being as weak as a wing. Instead it is as dangerous as an axe. With all these axes flailing both animals were getting badly gouged. That didn't matter so much in the case of the sea lion because, like the African lion, his hide is not good enough to be made into a fur coat. But in the case of the fur seal it was a serious matter, since the fur of this animal is almost as valuable as that of the sea otter.

The boys didn't care to mix into this fight and perhaps get killed.

'Where do these fur seals come from anyhow?' Roger wondered.

'From the Pribilof Islands up past Russia.'

'Russia! Why that's a million miles away.'

'No,' said Hal. 'The line between Russia and Alaska runs up through Bering Strait. If you walk out on the ice to that line and reach over and shake hands with somebody you are shaking hands with a Russian. Russia is as close as that to the United States.'

'If they were so close why didn't they grab Alaska?'

'They did just that. Peter the Great, Emperor of Russia, told Vitus Bering to find out what lay east of Siberia. Bering was the first white man to set foot upon Alaska. The young United States knew nothing about it. Canada knew nothing about it. The Russians took it over. Many years later they sold it to the United States for seven million dollars. Now it is worth billions instead of millions.'

Hal saw a black fin coming toward the two fighters.

'That's a killer whale,' he said. 'I'm afraid it's all

154

up with the lion and the bull. The killer whale has a keen appetite for seals and sea lions.'

But it was not all up. Frightened by the murderous whale, the two enemies quit fighting each other and prepared to face the killer whale. This was a battle they were not likely to win. If they ever needed help, this was the time.

Nanook was growling ferociously. He didn't like killer whales. He started toward the water and the boys let him go. The great bear swam out and sank his teeth into the lip of the killer. That gave courage to the lion and the bull and they joined Nanook in an attack upon the killer whale.

The killer would be killed himself if he didn't get away fast. He decided to seek his dinner elsewhere. With a swish of his great tail, he brushed his three tormentors toward the beach.

Nanook had so often seen the boys capture animals that he instinctively knew what to do. He pushed both animals up on to the beach. Hal promptly dropped the noose of his lasso over the head of the sea lion and Roger captured the fur seal in his net.

Hal said, 'We'll give them time for their nerves to quiet down a bit before we take them to the airport.'

'But won't they die — out of the water?'

'In ancient times', Hal said, 'they were both land animals. Even now they like to be out of the water just as well as in it.'

'But can they walk — without feet?'

'Their fins aren't quite as good as feet for walking,' admitted Hal, 'but they can waddle along. First, let them rest.'

The fur seal was looking at Roger with big, beautiful brown eyes.

'He looks as intelligent as the sea lion,' said Roger. 'And his face looks exactly like a bear's face.'

'You guessed it,' said Hal. 'He's a cousin of the bear. Steller called him a "sea bear".'

'How big he is!'

'I suppose he weighs about five hundred pounds. All the same, he can move fast. Look at those big strong shoulders and the lightning movements of his neck, and his big ivory teeth. They are like the teeth of a sperm whale. Notice how they curve back so that they can hang on to anything they close on. He has a terrific bite, and yet he never chews anything, just swallows it whole. Now he's beginning to dance around. That's the way fur seals are — very lively, full of fun.'

'Well,' said Roger, 'we'll have to give them the fun of a waddle to the airport.'

And waddle they did, with Nanook following close behind. The people of Barrow had never seen such a sight — a parade of two boys, two ferocious beasts, and the great white bear acting as policeman to see to it that these mighty fighters should waddle in peace to the airport.

27
The Whale That Sings
The Whale That
Whistles

'This is going to be a big day,' said Hal. 'Get on your Neoprene suit. We're going down.'

'What's up?' said Roger. 'I mean what's down?'

'The humpbacks and the belugas. A lot of both of them have just arrived. They are down there, waiting for us.'

'What are you talking about?'

'I'm talking about two kinds of whales that Dad wanted. They've just arrived from Hawaii — hundreds of them. The humpback is the most astonishing of all whales. You'll understand when you see him and hear him.'

'Hear a whale?' said Roger. 'Whales don't make any sound.'

'That's what you think,' said Hal. 'You'll put your fingers in your ears when the humpback sings. You've heard many sounds under water but nothing like the song of the humpback. So I've been told —

I've never heard it myself. This will be a new experience for both of us.'

'What did you say the other one was he wants us to get — a belly something?'

'Not belly. Beluga. It was named by the Russians. It comes from a Russian word meaning white. It's the only snow-white whale in the sea. It also is very musical.'

'Does it sing?' asked Roger.

'Not exactly. It whistles.'

When they came down, dressed in their rubber suits, the Eskimo landlord said, 'What are you after today?'

'Whales,' said Hal.

The landlord smiled. 'You are joking. Two boys against a whale! Everybody in town knows how smart you are. You have caught many animals. But when it comes to catching a whale — that's another matter. You probably don't even know the ceremony.'

'Ceremony?' Hal asked. 'What ceremony?'

'All the women of the town must close their mouths and keep quite silent. If they speak the whale will swim away. They must not move. If they do the whale will thrash about and escape. Also, for good luck, you must wear a magic charm with the picture of a whale on it. We Eskimos know these things.'

'I respect what you know,' said Hal. 'But perhaps all that ceremony is for Eskimos, not for us. Don't tell your women to keep quiet for our sake.'

'But you can't do this all alone.'

'No,' said Hal. 'We're going to have help. I saw the chief of the Coast Guard yesterday. They will have one of their big boats above us where we go down. If we get into trouble, they will help us. Anyhow, we're not after the big ones. The zoos would rather have young animals who have a long life ahead of them.'

'But even a young whale will be stronger than a dozen men. Even if you catch it, it will struggle and get away.'

'That's why we have this,' said Hal. He held a gun.

'You can't use that,' said the landlord. 'There's a law against killing whales.'

'I know,' said Hal. 'But this isn't to kill a whale. There's no powder in it — only a spring. Instead of firing a bullet it shoots a dart full of sleep medicine that will simply pierce the skin of the whale and put him to sleep.'

'You can't fool me,' said the landlord. 'A gun is a gun. And a gun kills. I'll have to tell our policeman what you are up to.'

'Go ahead,' said Hal. 'Perhaps he can help us.'

'He'll help you into the town jail.'

Hal smiled. 'Tell him first to talk to the captain of the Coast Guard. He knows that we're not interested in killing anything or anybody — even you. Now, if you will excuse us, we must get along.'

Hal and Roger walked to the Coast Guard station, where the men knew very well what the boys were up to and admired them for their courage.

A sleek, clean little vessel carried them around Point Barrow to the western side, where the water boiled with the frolicking whales. One monster who happened to be under the boat raised it up several feet into the air, where it teetered for a moment and then fell with a great splash into the sea.

The skipper said to Hal, 'How about it? Want to change your mind? There's a riot going on down there. You're taking an awful chance.'

'I don't think it will be too bad,' said Hal. 'Whales are not like sharks. They have no reason to attack us. By the way, where do you suppose they all came from?'

'From the warm waters down south. They spend the winter there. When summer comes it's too warm for them and they come up to the pleasant cool waters of the Arctic. Just as a precaution, give me the name and address of your folks so we can notify them if you get killed.'

Hal grinned. He didn't expect to get killed. But he gave the skipper what he had asked for. 'John Hunt, Hunt Wild Animal Farm, Long Island, New York.'

The boys adjusted the scubas on their backs, then stepped over the starboard gunwhale and sank into the water.

The peaceful giants made room for them. They gathered around in a great circle and sang. Hal had never heard such a song before. Roger could not believe his ears. The gentle monsters let loose with an underwater concert such as the boys had never heard in any opera house.

Some of the notes slid from high to low like a police siren. Some were trilled, some were burbled. Sometimes there was a distinct melody. Some sang soprano, some mezzo-soprano, some alto and some bass.

Underneath it all was a boom-boom like the sound of big drums and the rat-a-tat-tat of snare drums. The big whales thundered, the little ones squeaked. Music boomed, echoed, swelled, a medley of glorious sound. It was a fanfare of trumpets, trombones, clarinets, oboes, bassoons, saxophones and flutes — not to mention the deep thunder of the pipe organ.

Since it came from huge lungs, the roar was deafening.

Hal remembered that the *National Geographic* had published a recording of the songs of humpback whales. And now they were listening to the whales themselves doing even better than the record.

But what was that whistling sound? Somebody or something was whistling a tune. Hal pointed to a smaller whale all in white. It was one of the belugas, sometimes called white whales. Evidently it could not sing, but it whistled its heart out.

Why were the humpbacks called humpbacks? Like the killer whale, which carries a fin on its back projecting upward about five feet sharp and strong, the humpback also has a fin on its back but quite different in appearance. It was low and thick and looked more like a lump than a fin. And some had no lump at all.

The humpback was oddly shaped. Hal could understand why it was called the most remarkable of all whales. It had an enormous head and its jaws when open were big enough to swallow a Jonah. Its two swimming fins were unusually long. Its various parts were awkwardly joined together like the segments of an ant. The front section was huge, but then the body tapered down to a narrow tail.

It went through all sorts of crazy movements. It loved to stand on its head with its tail projecting up out of the water. It could curl up like a doughnut. It would furiously splash the water with the large flukes of its tail. And all the time it sang as lustily as the calliope on a Mississippi steamboat.

The big ones were 50 feet long. Hal had read that the heart alone of such a monster weighs 430 pounds. The young ones, who were singing high soprano, were about 12 feet long. Even they weighed about 3,000 pounds. Hal, picking out one of them that looked good to him, used his sleep gun. The dart penetrated the young one's skin. The sleep medicine circulated through its body. It had not been hurt in the least but it quit singing and drifted lazily to the surface. A hawser was cast from the deck of the vessel and Hal looped it around the neck of the whale.

So far, so good. Now they must get a beluga. Roger straddled the back of one of the white beauties and Hal gave it a shot of sleep. The men on the Coast Guard boat laughed when they saw Roger and the whale pop up out of the water.

Roger caught the rope thrown to him and put the noose over this sleeping beauty.

The boys climbed aboard and the two sleeping whales were towed around the Point to the airport, where airfield employees loaded them into tanks for the flight south. The cargo plane left at once in order to get to Long Island before their big passengers woke up.

The boys returned to their lodging house. The landlord laughed.

'So, you had to give up,' he said. 'I knew you couldn't do it. The women moved and talked and you didn't wear any whale charm, so, of course, you failed.'

Hal smiled. 'I hope we fail as badly every time,' he said.

28
A Sheep Can Kill

They were climbing a mountain of the Brooks Range. It was difficult because the ground was covered with slippery snow.

Behind them was a sledge, pulled not by a dog team but by a boy team. The two boys did not mind much since it was light and there was nothing much on it but a folded-up tent and some provisions.

But an icy wind was blowing. The higher they went, the colder they got.

Roger stopped and beat his mittened hands together to get them warm. 'It's as cold as Greenland,' he complained.

'We feel it more than we did there because we are climbing,' Hal said.

Every time they inhaled the cold air they shivered. It was hard to breathe. The deadly chill started at the feet and went up through the body, numbing the stomach, the kidneys, the heart, turning the nose and chin white with frostbite.

'What did we come here for anyhow?' Roger demanded.

'To get a sheep,' said Hal.

Roger stared at his brother. 'You mean we're going through all this just to get a sheep?'

'Not the kind of sheep you're thinking about,' said Hal. 'We're not after the sort of sheep the farmer has in his pasture.'

'Is there any other kind?'

'There sure is. I'm hoping to find a bighorn. It's twice as big as a farmer's sheep. It's strong and wild and dangerous.'

'Why do they call it a bighorn?'

'Its horns are the heaviest part of it. They are thick and solid and they go around in a complete circle. One bunt of that great horny head and you are done for.'

Roger's sharp eyes saw something moving. 'It's a man — a man with a gun.'

Hal said, 'Wherever there's a man with a gun there is trouble.'

'He's coming this way,' said Roger.

The man who joined them was a heavily built brute, with a mean face and a mean gun.

When he joined them he said, 'Hello you guys. I'll bet we're after the same thing. A bighorn. Sorry to disappoint you, but if we see one, I'll be the one to get it. You see, I'm a sharpshooter.'

'Where are you from?' Hal asked.

'Wyoming. I'm a bit famous down there. Perhaps you've heard of me. My name is Alec.'

Hal at once thought of the term 'Smart Alec', which according to the dictionary was applied to anyone who was a braggart and felt himself very clever.

'Sorry to meet you,' said Hal with a smile. 'I'm afraid we'd better give up right now.'

'Well,' said Smart Alec, 'you can tag along if you like and see how I operate. It will be a good lesson for you — to see how an expert does these things.'

'I'm sure we will learn a lot,' said Hal. 'Just why do you want to kill a bighorn?'

'To put the head and horns up on the wall in my house. I already have the living-room wall covered with antlers, but I think there's perhaps room for one more.'

'So you've done a lot of killing,' said Hal.

'Killing is my middle name. I'm afraid of nothing that walks. Why should I be afraid of a dall sheep? That's another name, you know, for a bighorn.'

'You may find', said Hal gently, 'that the dall is no doll.'

'Never mind. I don't care what it is. The worse it is, the better I'll like it. I always get away pretty well with a tough job. After all, the Bible says man is superior to any beast.'

'When did you last read your Bible?'

'I don't read it. Somebody told me. And he was right. No animal on earth is as good as me.'

Hal said, 'How about the ones that have sharper eyesight than any man, sharper hearing, better sense of smell, don't go to war and kill millions of their own kind? They don't smoke themselves into cancer and they don't get drunk. They don't neglect their young ones as some human parents do and don't go around shooting men in order to put their heads up on the wall.'

'I can see that you're a couple of mollycoddles,' said Alec. 'I'll go along with you to protect you from the sheep. You'd never make it alone.'

Hal noticed that the stranger had given his own name, but didn't bother to learn the names of the two he had met. He was thinking only of himself.

They proceeded up the mountain. Since Alaska is farther south than the polar part of Greenland, the sun was much higher than it had been in the far north, and stronger. Its reflection on the snow was painful and the three began to feel as if they had sand in their eyes, or hot knives. They were in danger of going snow blind. Roger began to wish that they were animals who didn't mind the glare.

Hal had known beforehand that their eyes would suffer.

He drew out of his pocket a piece of walrus hide and some string.

'Wait a moment,' he said. 'We'll have to make three pairs of goggles.' He cut out three strips two inches wide and about seven inches long. He put one of the strips over Roger's eyes.

'What's that for?' asked Roger. 'Now I can't see a thing.'

'I just wanted to find out if it was a good fit,' said Hal. 'Now I'll finish the job.'

He took the strip and cut two slits in it, one for each eye. Then he put the strip back over Roger's eyes and tied it fast around his head with the string.

Now Roger could see through the slits and the glare was gone.

'Now I'll make one for you,' Hal said to Smart Alec.

But Alec would have none of that. 'What do you think I am, a child? Don't try to baby me or I'll punch you on the nose.'

'O.K.,' said Hal, 'but I'll baby myself.' And he made a pair of walrus goggles and put them on. He could see through the slits, but there was no longer any sun-pain. 'You'd better let me make one for you,' he said to Alec.

But Smart Alec was indignant. 'That's all right for kids,' he said. 'I mean, if you have weak eyes. Mine are strong. I'm no weakling.'

He trudged on, with his eyes almost closed. Now and then he stumbled. He was evidently suffering intense pain. Hal felt sorry for the boob. He knew that the eyes of Smartypants must feel as if they were full of needles. Alec could hardly see where he was going. Hal took his arm, but Smart Alec shook him off. He was a fool, and a fool is too proud to accept help.

They came upon a small herd of caribou. Most of them passed by, but one big bull stopped and pawed the ground angrily. He had magnificent horns reaching above his head four feet high. Hal had seen plenty of caribou, but none like this king of the snows.

Smart Alec could also see the towering horns. 'I've got to have those antlers,' he said and prepared to shoot.

Before he could do so, the bull lowered his horns, drove them into Alec's stomach, and lifted him twelve feet high. Now Smart Alec did not sound very smart. He howled with pain. No wonder, with those sharp prongs slicing through his hide.

Hal wanted to do something to help, but before he could think what to do, the bull started off with the herd. Every time he put his foot down with a jolt, the Smartie yelled blue murder as the sharp points dug further into his anatomy.

The climax came when the bull stopped at the edge of a cliff and dropped him twenty feet into a snowbank, screaming as he fell.

Hal went and helped him up. Alec was crying. 'I'm full of holes,' he said. 'Got to have some antiseptic. Those antlers have poisoned me. I'll get gangrene and die.'

'No you won't,' said Hal. 'Those antlers are as clean as a surgeon's knife. They're always up in the clean air — never get dirty — except that now they have some of your dirty blood.'

'How come you know so much about animals?' said Alec.

'It's my business,' Hal said. 'Now pull up your coat and your shirt and let's see what's happening.'

The skin was punctured here and there and blood was oozing out. But as soon as it reached the surface it froze solid and stopped the bleeding. So the frigid climate did what a doctor could not do.

Smart Alec did not feel very peppy. 'I want to go home.'

'Perk up,' said Hal. 'You're not badly hurt. Don't forget — we're after a bighorn.'

They came upon one an hour later. It stood proudly on a big rock. It was a magnificent fellow with great heavy horns that curled around and came back to where they had started. Smart Alec raised his gun. Smarter Hal had just brushed away the snow and picked up a small pebble. He threw it at the bighorn and when it struck the animal moved a few feet and the bullet missed.

All Alec had done was just annoy the animal and it now stood up on its hind feet and came toward him. It was taller than he was, and a great deal stronger.

Hal brought out his sleep gun. 'I thought you didn't believe in guns,' said Alec.

'I believe in this one,' said Hal, and he fired.

The dart pierced the skin of the big sheep. He came down on all four feet and began scratching at the dart. He got it loose but the medicine had already gone into his body and was at work. Since he could wander away before the sleep medicine took effect, Hal lassoed him and held fast.

Roger drew the sledge up beside the animal. When the dall began to teeter Hal pushed it over and tied it fast on the sledge.

'Well, you won that round,' said Alec. 'By the way, what's your name?'

Hal told him.

Alec looked at him with more interest than he had shown before. 'I saw something in the papers about you. You take animals for zoos.'

'That's right,' said Hal. 'What's your business in Wyoming?'

'I have a ranch. Wyoming has some wild life too. And a fair number of zoos. I've a notion to imitate you — but on a small scale. Perhaps we can pick up some animals alive for our zoos.'

'That's the best thing you've said yet,' said Hal. 'Good luck to you.'

They parted on good terms. The Hunts with their trophy went down to the mountain's base, where a truck waited to take them to Point Barrow.

29
The Moose and the Mouse

'Send me the biggest moose you can find,' John Hunt telegraphed to his sons.

Hal knew where to find the largest moose in the whole world. 'This means a trip to the Kenai Peninsula,' he said.

'I know where that is,' said Roger. 'But it's too far away. We're on the north edge of Alaska. Kenai is on the south edge. Aren't there moose right around here somewhere?'

'There are moose in many parts of Alaska, but the really great ones are the Kenai moose. That's where we'll have to go to find the big boys.'

Early the next morning they were on the plane that would carry them south from the Arctic Ocean to an even greater ocean, the Pacific. They knew the pilot and co-pilot because they had so often visited the Point Barrow airport to arrange for shipment of their animals to Long Island.

'Hope you enjoy the trip,' said the pilot, Ben Bolt. 'If you want to come up in the cockpit now and then it will be quite all right. You can get a better view there of what's ahead.'

What was ahead was quite thrilling. First the plane had to soar ten thousand feet high to clear the mountains of the Brooks Range. Then down, only to rise again to get over the Endicott Mountains.

Over dozens of lakes, then up again to cross the Ray Mountains.

Now below them was the great Yukon River. They were no sooner over that than they must climb again over the Mooseheart Mountains.

Then came the most thrilling experience. They passed over Mount McKinley National Park. They flew close to Mount McKinley, highest mountain in North America, but did not attempt to fly over it. They did fly above the other mountains of the Park, Mount Brooks, Mount Hunter and Mount Foraker.

Then over lakes, lakes, lakes — what a wet country Alaska was! Over a great glacier, over Cook Inlet, then down to the airport in the small town of Kenai.

Hal and Roger were in the cockpit when a big moose appeared in the middle of the runway. The moose is a proud animal, and very stubborn. He does not make way for anybody. Everybody must make way for him. He rules the animal kingdom in the north, just as the elephant in Africa is all-powerful. There, if you see an elephant in the road, you must stop and wait — perhaps for hours — because elephants 'have the right of way'. In Alaska 'moose have the right of way'.

The moose continued to stand there as solid as a rock while the plane rushed toward him. The pilot

174

did his best to bring the plane to a halt. It was no use. Plane and moose met with a sickening crunch. The whirling propeller tried to turn the moose into a hamburger. The plane came to a sudden stop throwing everyone forward. The moose must have been badly hurt, but no sound came from him because a moose does not cry as lesser animals may do.

Airport hands helped to disentangle propeller and moose, then turned the plane about and let it move slowly to another runway. In the meantime the moose remained exactly where he had been just as if he were not a living animal, but a granite statue.

'Now you get an idea', said Ben, 'of what a job you are going to have if you try to capture a moose.'

'That one wasn't big enough,' said Hal. 'Where can we find a really great one?'

'At Moose Pass,' said Ben. 'But first you'd better have lunch with us and we'll tell you what you are up against. You may change your mind about trying to capture a moose.'

As they ate Ben told them what he had learned about this animal during his twenty-five years in Alaska.

'Right here you will find the biggest moose on earth,' said Ben. 'There are moose in Europe, but there they call them elk and they are about half the size of the Alaskan moose. The bull moose in Kenai weighs about eighteen hundred pounds and is much taller than any horse. Up to the top of his horns he may measure as much as twelve feet.'

Hal looked up. 'This room measures about eight feet from floor to ceiling,' he said. 'The moose is

175

four feet taller! No wonder he's the animal king of Alaska.'

'The moose belongs to the deer family,' said Ben. 'But did you ever see any antlers on a deer as wide as these — six feet across? He puts about fifty pounds of food every day into his stomach.'

'What kind of food?' Roger asked.

'Wood,' said Ben. 'He doesn't kill any animals. He eats no meat. He eats trees — the leaves, twigs, even the trunks. The Indian name for him is *musee*, which means wood-eater. From *musee* we get the word moose.'

'You mentioned Moose Pass,' said Hal. 'Do we fly there?'

'No. You had better hire a wanigan.'

'What in heaven's name is a wanigan?'

'It's a sort of van. It is usually pulled by a tractor. When it is used on snow it has runners. But there's no snow here, so it is fitted with wheels and it has a motor of its own. You'll have to have a wanigan to bring back your moose — if you get one. I'll take you to a wanigan garage.'

The boys rented a wanigan, said goodbye to their aviator friends, and set out on the road to Moose Pass.

Half-way there they encountered a moose. Of course he stood in the middle of the road. Remembering that moose have the right of way, Hal stopped the wanigan. For half an hour they waited. Some men were working at the side of the road. One of them called, 'I'll move him for you.'

He picked up a stone and threw it. It struck the moose on his nose. The nose of a moose is like no other nose on earth. It is a foot long, and very tender. The animal uses it as if it were a hand. The nose picks leaves from a tree and stuffs them into the mouth. It is the moose's pride and joy and he resents any interference with it.

This moose got the idea that the stone had come from the wanigan. He did not stay still one moment longer. He came bellowing and snorting like a steam engine.

Hal backed the wanigan down the road but the angry moose, with a speed that one would not expect from so large a beast, overtook the car. A moose is accustomed to standing on his hind feet to reach high branches. This time he stood on his hind feet, and with his powerful front feet pushed the wanigan over into the ditch. There it lay upside down with its engine still whirring. The upside-down boys crawled out and retreated into a field. The moose, having punished those he considered his tormentors, wandered away, his big nose trembling with anger.

The road men were Eskimos and, true to their nature, came at once to help. Together with the boys, they got the wanigan right side up and back on the road. The boys, feeling a little shaken, thanked the men and went on their way.

Eventually they came to a point where the railroad crossed the road, and near by was a small railway station. They went in to rest and get any information they could from the station master. On the wall they saw a sign which read, 'NOT RESPONSIBLE FOR ANY DELAYS CAUSED BY MOOSE.'

'You boys want a ticket?' said the station master.
'No,' said Hal. 'We just came in to get some

information about moose. We noticed the sign on the wall. Evidently you have trouble with moose getting on the track.'

'Yes,' said the old station master. 'We've killed a lot of them. You've come to the right place for information. I know about all there is to know about the moose. It's a very strong animal, and if you eat it it makes you strong. The left hind foot of a moose is a cure for epilepsy. Bones from the antlers will take away headache. If you grind part of an antler up into powder it will be an antidote for snakebite. The hoof of a moose will cure six hundred diseases.'

A young man who had heard all this laughed. 'The old geezer has a lot of superstitions,' he said.

Hal said, 'But the moose is really a very remarkable animal.'

'Yes it is. It is born with its eyes wide open. Seven days after birth it can outrun a man. The female adult moose weighs a thousand pounds and the bull moose weighs almost twice as much. Its antlers are unique. They look like big soup plates. With its terrific front feet it can trample to death bears, wolves, cougars, coyotes and wolverines. You wouldn't imagine it could get so strong eating nothing but asters, ferns, lilies, duckweed, burrweed, duck potato and all kinds of wood. It also eats the leaves and twigs of aspen, balsam, birch, maple and mountain ash. It's so big and clumsy-looking, yet it can slip through the woods without a sound. In spite of its diet of lilies and such it can get very dangerous. It crashes headlong into cars and yesterday one charged a locomotive. That was a bit too much for His Majesty.'

178

'He died?'

'Yes, he died. But there are plenty more. Are you especially interested in moose?'

'Just now, yes,' said Hal. 'We want to take one alive for a zoo.'

'It would be easier to take one dead.'

Hal laughed. 'I don't think we'll try to pick up the bones along the railroad tracks. Where are the live ones?'

'A good place to find them is around Kenai Lake. I'll go with you if you like.'

'Great. My name is Hal. This is Roger, my brother.'

'I'm Ivak — part Eskimo, part Montana.'

The wanigan bumped over a fair road to the lake. Sure enough, there were several big bulls here, some on shore, some in the water. With them were some cow moose. They were smaller than the bulls, and had no horns. Also there were calves, hornless as yet, but bright, lively and strong.

'You notice', said Ivak, 'that nearly all of them are inside that big circle where the grass is trampled down. That is called a mooseyard. Where there are many moose, you'll always find a mooseyard. It's a sort of meeting place, where they get together and enjoy each other's company. And they don't like to have any other animal come in and try to join the club.'

'What magnificent antlers they have,' said Hal. 'They don't go up very much like the antlers of a deer. They go out — one set from the right side of the head, and the other from the left. Each one looks like a huge platter or a soup tureen. How would you describe them?'

Ivak said, 'To me they look like big shovels. They can carry things on those enormous plates.'

'What kind of things?' Roger asked.

'Bushes, plants, weeds — anything they want to eat later on. And you notice they have a fence all around the plate to hold things in.'

'You mean that row of spikes? They look sharp and dangerous.'

'They are the weapons of the moose. If any enemy comes around, the moose lowers its head and plunges those spikes into it and kills it. You see that some have only a few spikes, perhaps a dozen — and others may have as many as forty — all of them as sharp as needles.'

'Why is there so much difference?' Roger asked.

'Nature plays tricks,' said Ivak. 'One moose is not exactly like another. They are like people — all different. Just as a lady may wear a different hairdo, so each moose has a different horn-do.'

'What are those moose doing out in the lake?'

'Watch and you will see them disappear beneath the surface. They go down after water plants. They scrape up the plants with their horns. There's one that has just come up. He has a load of plants on his platters. When he is ready to eat them he will shake the plants off on to the ground and use his long nose to push them into his mouth.'

'Look!' said Roger. 'There's a grizzly. He's coming right into the mooseyard.'

'That's very bad manners', said Ivak, 'for any

other animal to burst into the private club of the moose. He'll get what he deserves.'

A huge bull moose was attacked by the grizzly. Every grizzly thinks himself very important. He is used to conquering any animal who interferes with him. This grizzly stood up on his hind feet in order to get his teeth into the neck of the moose. All he got was the goatee or whiskers that hung from the moose's throat. He spat these out and tried again.

If a grizzly bear can stand on its hind feet, so can a moose. The moose stood erect, battered the bear's face with his front feet as a boxer does with his fists. But the rock-hard hooves of the moose were much more terrible than the gloved fists of a boxer.

The grizzly who had invaded the private domain of the moose was thoroughly punished. His face looked like a bowl of mush. Still he fought. Evidently more severe measures were necessary to punish this rascal. The moose lowered his head and used the deadly spikes on his antlers to punch his enemy full of holes.

The impudent grizzly, who probably never before had met an enemy he could not conquer, fell away and crawled out of the mooseyard.

'I think that's the moose we want,' said Hal. 'He's the biggest one of the lot.'

Ivak grinned. 'Do you think you can do better than the grizzly?'

'Yes,' said Hal, 'but without fighting.'

'This is something I want to see,' said Ivak. 'Perhaps you are going to use your lasso.'

'No,' said Hal. 'The lasso is no good in this case. He would break it.'

'Then you are going to use gentle persuasion? You won't get far with that.'

'We'll see,' said Hal. 'Roger, do your bit and I'll do mine.' He went outside the magic circle, where he had seen a hole made by field mice. He stepped very softly, not wishing to alarm any mouse that might be at home. He lay down beside the hole and waited.

In the meantime, Roger was doing his bit. He walked slowly toward the giant moose. The moose had learned to be afraid of guns, but this visitor had no gun. He had no pistol, no stick, no knife. The great moose, master of the mountains, was not in the habit of running from anybody or anything — except a gun.

Roger came close and began speaking in soft tones. It was a friendly voice and the speaker was only a boy, so what was there to be afraid of? He let the boy pat his great neck.

182

Hal came, carrying in his hand a wriggling mouse. He walked very slowly, keeping his hands out in full sight so that the moose would understand that he had no gun. Then, very gently, he placed the mouse on the foot-long nose of the moose.

The little eyes of the mouse studied the moose, and the great eyes of the moose were fixed upon the mouse.

Neither was afraid of the other. By a dip of his nose, the giant could have slipped the mouse into his mouth and swallowed it.

He did not, for several reasons. First, the mouse was too small to do him any harm. Second, he never ate other animals. He was a strict vegetarian. He ate no meat. But the main reason was that he had never before been visited by a friendly little mouse. It was quite evident that he liked the little beast.

The mouse crawled up the nose and on up into the antlers, where he lay down in the soup bowl or shovel or platter or whatever one might want to call it. Some leaves remained in the bowl and they happened to be to his liking. He munched on them and was very happy. This was better than a hole in the ground.

But a mouse can never stay still for very long. The little fellow noticed the wanigan. He crawled out of the shovel, and down the nose, and dropped to the ground. He also had a nose but nothing in comparison with the nose of the great moose. The mouse's nose, though small, was very keen and he smelled some food that the boys had left in the wanigan. He went in to investigate.

The great moose stood for a long time gazing at

the wanigan. He was evidently waiting for his small friend to come out.

When he did not, the moose walked slowly to the wanigan and looked inside. After thinking it over, he climbed up into the wanigan making the floor creak under his weight of almost a ton.

Hal, very quietly, let down the sliding door at the back of the wanigan. Before it completely closed Roger thrust in a big bush for the wood-eater to dine upon during the trip to Kenai airport.

The boys thanked Ivak for his help, then climbed into the cab, which was separated by a partition from the quarters occupied by the moose and the mouse. They drove back to the Kenai airport and made arrangements for the transport of the mighty moose to Long Island and, on the next day, flew back to Point Barrow and their faithful Nanook.

30
The Wild Williwaw

They were climbing Castle Mountain when the williwaw caught them.

'I'm afraid we're in for it,' Hal said. 'Here comes a williwaw.'

'What kind of an animal is a williwaw?' Roger asked.

'It's not a wild beast,' said Hal. 'It's a wild storm. It's a hurricane and a typhoon and a tornado all mixed up together. It's born in the Aleutian Islands and it sweeps across Alaska tearing down houses and killing cattle.'

'Doesn't sound too good,' said Roger. 'What can we do about it?'

'Nothing much. Just try to stay alive. Lucky we didn't bring our big tent. It would be blown away. The pup tent we brought will be better.'

'Let's get it up in a hurry,' said his young brother.

You don't carry anything more than you have to when you climb a mountain. The pup tent was light and small. It was just long enough for the one sleeping bag they had brought. The bag was large enough for two, providing that you didn't mind being jammed together like a couple of sardines.

They anchored the tent to the ground with large rocks. Surely the wind wouldn't be strong enough to blow away 100-pound rocks.

Hal had wisely placed the tent with its back end toward the wind.

'That's about all we can do,' he said. 'See those black clouds racing in from the west? They're full of wind. Let's get inside.'

They crawled into the pup tent. Hal laced the flaps securely.

'You get into the bag first,' he said. 'Then I'll try to squeeze in beside you.'

The wind struck with the force of a thousand hammers. The pup tent was ripped loose and sailed away toward Canada. The rocks on the side toward the wind rolled in upon the sleeping bag.

'Ouch!' cried Roger. 'Get off my chest.'

'I'm not on your chest,' said Hal. 'That's just a couple of hundred pounds of rock.'

'Why did you pile them on me?'

'The wind did that without my help. Just be patient. The wind will blow them away again.'

The next gust picked them up and carried them off as if they had been cardboard boxes instead of rocks.

'I suppose we'll go next,' said Roger.

'Perhaps not. We're heavier than rocks. This rock weighed about one hundredweight. You and I together weigh about three hundred pounds.'

To make matters worse, the black cloud sent down a deluge of rain. The bag was waterproof, so the boys pulled its flap over their heads.

'It can rain all it pleases,' said Hal. 'We're snug and warm.'

But the rain soon turned into hail. The hailstones were as big as the biggest marbles.

'They're knocking the breath out of me,' complained Roger.

'Lie face down,' said Hal. 'Then your lungs will be protected.'

It was no easy matter to twist into a face-down position. Hal got a few smart blows from the elbows of his squirming brother. He himself had a stronger rib cage and could stand the pummelling he got from the bullets of the sky. He put his arm over his face.

The wind was roaring and screeching like a banshee. How long would this go on? Hal didn't know the habits of a williwaw. He had heard that the willies, as the Alaskans call them, came rushing down the valleys and mountainsides like devils bent on destroying everything man had made. If any planes were in the sky they would not remain there. They would be dashed to pieces against the mountain peaks.

Surely, he thought, this furious blizzard could not last long. It would peter out before evening and they would be home in time to have a good night's sleep.

But the williwaw had no intention of petering out. It became worse as night arrived and it continued until daybreak.

'I'm hungry,' said Roger.

Hal said, 'I'm afraid you'll just have to stay hungry. We didn't bring any food because we expected to be in Barrow for supper.'

187

Roger was angry. 'You were a big boob not to bring anything to eat.'

'O.K.,' said Hal. 'I was a big boob. Perhaps you were a little boob because you didn't think of it.'

'Why should I think of it? You're the boss.'

'Sometimes I think you are,' said Hal. 'You're fifteen. It's time you started to think for yourself.'

'I'd punch you on the nose if I could get my hand loose.'

Hal laughed. 'What are we getting into? You and I never quarrel. It's this blooming storm that is getting us down. Getting our nerves on edge.'

Thunder and lightning joined the wind and the hail. And it was getting icy cold. Two days and two nights went by without food and without any pause in the violent storm.

Then the wind died, the whirling dervishes in the sky quit putting on their act and the boys emerged from their cocoon. They could hardly walk about, so cramped and stiff were their legs and so empty their stomachs.

The storm had wiped out the trail they had come by. The sky remained covered with cloud so the sun could give them no help. East, west, north, south, did not exist for them. They were completely lost.

'Someone will come along,' was Roger's optimistic forecast. No one came along.

'At least we have to go down the mountain,' said Hal. 'We know that much.'

'Yes, which way down?' Castle Mountain was only 3,700 feet high and they were at the top. Every way down but one would be a mistake.

With so many mistakes possible, it was not surprising that they stumbled at random down the rocks, hoping against hope that they would meet some human being. They met a bear, but he could tell them nothing. He didn't even try to eat them because he had already dined and these scrawny, starved humans didn't look like a good dinner.

They sat down occasionally, puffing and snorting and trying to get their strength and their breath back. Hal wished that he could carry Roger, but the boy would resent being carried like a baby and, besides, Hal was much too weak to carry 130 pounds in his arms or on his back.

Then they saw it — a cabin!

'Whoever lives there', Hal said, 'will help us. We can get warm by his fire and he may even let us have a little food. What luck!'

The roof was covered with half-melted hail three or four inches thick. The walls were made of heavy logs that were too stout to have been destroyed by the storm. The furious wind had caved in one window.

Hal knocked at the door. There was no answer. He rapped again. Nothing doing. Roger was shaking with cold. He sat down on the steps.

Hal said, 'The fellow who lives here must have gone to town.'

Looking at Roger he thought, 'I must get him in and warm him up. If I don't, he'll get pneumonia.'

He climbed in through the broken window, cutting himself with some of the loose bits of glass. He stepped down on to a table and from that to the floor. What a relief to be in a house again, even one so small as this.

He called. There was no answer. There was no one in the cabin but himself.

'Come in through the window, Roger. There's nobody home and the door is solidly locked.'

Roger came in, scratching himself as Hal had done. He looked about. 'Isn't this great. We'll start a fire and perhaps we'll even find some food. Do you think the owner would mind?'

'I don't think there is any owner,' said Hal. 'It's been cleaned out completely. The door isn't really locked. It's just been jammed shut by the years.' He shivered. 'It's as cold as a refrigerator. It doesn't even have a stove. All the dishes are gone, pots, pans, everything.'

'Well, anyhow, it's ours for the time being,' said Roger. 'Isn't that the custom in the North? An empty house is for anybody. Isn't that the way it goes?'

'That's right,' said Hal. 'But it isn't of much use to us without food and without a stove.'

'What are those tin cans in the corner? Piled up on each other. There's a sort of pipe going up through the ceiling. I'll bet the person who made it thinks that he made a stove. Let's try it.'

'We have to have wood,' said Hal, 'and there's not a stick in the cabin.'

'But there was a sort of hump that I had to stand on to get in through the window. It's all covered with hail, but I'll bet there's some wood beneath,' said Roger.

'Bright idea,' said Hal. 'Let's heave open this door. It's just stuck.'

They threw their combined weight against the door and it popped open.

Roger attacked the hump with his mittened hands. He cleared away the hail. 'There's a cord of wood here,' he exclaimed. 'Do you think he forgot it?'

'Perhaps. But it's more likely that he left it on purpose for anybody who wanted to use the cabin. People up here are like that.'

They took some sticks inside and Hal whittled off some shavings with his pocket knife.

He put the shavings in the silly tin stove, put some sticks on top, and blessed the tin stove when the fire blazed up and began to warm the room.

It was wonderful to feel even the small heat from this stove. They began to feel human once more. Roger's stiff joints relaxed.

'Now, if we only had some food. I'll bet there's some somewhere. The last people who were here left the wood and surely they would have left something to eat.'

'Well,' said Hal, 'you can look for it if you like, while I patch up that window. We won't get very warm with a busted window.'

'There's no way you can patch it up,' said Roger. 'There's not a towel in the house, not an old shirt, not a piece of board, nothing.'

While Roger started his search for food Hal went outside. He faced an almost impossible task. If there had been snow he would have cut out a block of it and wedged it into the open space left by the broken window. But there was no snow. There was plenty of ice on the ground formed from hail that had frozen together into flat slabs. With his knife he cut out a section of hail-made ice and fitted it over the hole in the window.

Then he went in, expecting Roger to congratulate him. Instead Roger said, 'That's no good. The heat from the stove will melt it.'

'It will try to,' said Hal, 'but perhaps the chill air from outside will keep the ice from melting. We've seen ice windows in Greenland. They last for months. There's heat inside but the cold outside is stronger than the heat.'

'I'll bet your window will melt,' said Roger, 'and it will be as cold as Greenland inside here.'

But the window did not melt and the tin stove gave off enough heat to keep them half comfortable.

'I found some food,' said Roger.

'You did? That's great. You're not such a dumb cluck after all. What kind of food?'

'Pemmican, and dried raisins, some pretty tired bread, and a can of milk frozen solid. May I serve you? Do you like your milk hard or soft?'

'Soft, if you please.'

'Very well, sir,' said Roger. 'I shall put the milk on the stove and you shall have your milk not only thawed soft, but hot. Can you think of any greater luxury than that?'

When they had eaten Hal smacked his lips. 'The best restaurant in New York couldn't have done better,' he said.

Next morning the sun shone and they could tell which way was north. They went down the mountain to the river at its base. There was no bridge in sight. But there was hardly any water in the river.

'We'll have to walk across,' said Hal. 'We'll only get our feet wet.'

On his second step Hal's right leg suddenly sank

from sight. The other leg followed. He was terrified. He realized suddenly that he was facing death.

'Stay where you are,' he shouted to Roger.

'What's the trouble?'

'Quicksand!'

He did everything possible to free his legs. But he couldn't get either leg loose. Every moment he was sinking further. Roger started out to help him. 'Stay where you are,' commanded Hal. 'No use both of us getting caught.'

Now the sand was up to his waist. He writhed and squirmed. The sand soaked with icy water was chilling him to the bone.

'Lie down,' Roger shouted.

This seemed to Hal a ridiculous thing to say. Why should he lie down? Well, of course, if he lay down there would be so much of him on top of the sand that he might not sink more. It was worth a try. He lay flat upon the sand, and worked to get his legs loose. He was more dead than alive. He was cold and exhausted but he kept struggling until his whole body including the legs lay flat on the sand.

Then he began inching toward the land. With a final struggle he reached firm ground. He lay on the shore breathing hard, his heart going like a trip-hammer. His clothes were soaked and heavy and his caribou boots were full of sand and water. He felt he couldn't move an inch.

Roger knelt and took Hal's head in his hands.

'Don't be in a hurry,' he said. 'This is as good a place to rest as any.' Kneeling in sand and water, he was as dirty as his brother.

So Hal rested for half an hour. Then he got up

and staggered off with Roger, looking for a bridge. It was almost dark before they found one.

After they had crossed it a car going their way pulled up in front of them. The Eskimo driver had seen that these staggering, soaking wet, sand-pasted fellows were in need of help.

'Where are you going?' he said.

'To Barrow village,' Hal answered.

'Hop in,' said the Eskimo. 'If there's any hop left in you.'

'Mighty little,' laughed Hal. And with the little hop he had left he climbed into the car.

Arriving in Barrow, he heartily thanked the Eskimo driver for his kindness, and with Roger's support he wobbled over to their lodging, where the proprietor stood in the door. He did not recognize Hal and said sharply, 'This is a respectable place. We don't take any bums here.'

Roger said, 'Don't you recognize us? We're the Hunts.'

'Oh, a thousand pardons.' And he admitted these smelly, wet, dirty 'bums' to his proud establishment, which was almost as dirty as the 'bums'.

31
Orchestra of the Elks

A telegram came from their father.

YOU ARE DOING GOOD WORK. WE COULD USE
ALASKAN ELK WHITE GRIZZLY GIANT KODIAK.

Hal went to the airport and showed the telegram
to his pilot friend, Ben Bolt.

'The best place to find those animals', said Ben,
'is down in that wonderful country called the Valley
of Ten Thousand Smokes.'

'I've heard of it,' said Hal. 'That's where one of
the volcanoes exploded and sent clouds of smoke and
gas around the world.'

'One of the two biggest eruptions in all history,'
said Ben. 'The other was Krakatoa.'

'But isn't it still dangerous there?'

'Perhaps. But danger never stopped you.'

'And we can find elk there?'

'Quite near there,' said Ben. 'Most of them are on
Afognak Island. It's just across the strait from the
volcanoes. I can't take you there because there's no
landing strip. But I can fly you and Nanook to the
volcano country and you can get a boat across to

Afognak. Almost touching that island is another called Kodiak Island and that's where you will find the biggest and strongest bear in all creation, the Kodiak bear. How you will ever bag that ferocious monster I can't imagine, but that's up to you.'

'And how about grizzlies?'

'You'll find them almost anywhere. Or they'll find you. They have a grudge against all two-legged animals such as you and your brother.'

Hal said, 'Our father wants us to get a white grizzly. I thought all grizzlies were grey.'

'Most of them are,' said Ben. 'But he means the silver-tip.'

'Just what is a silver-tip?'

'The tip of every hair is a silvery white so it looks as if the bear is wearing a white coat. A silver-tip is a very dangerous animal. It looks beautiful, but it has a devil where its heart should be. You'd better carry a gun.'

Hal laughed. 'I don't think Dad would appreciate a dead grizzly.'

'O.K. It's your funeral,' said Ben. 'When will you be ready to go?'

'Tomorrow morning. Eight o'clock. All right by you?'

'Fine. I'll be ready.'

The next morning after breakfast Hal paid the proprietor, who said, 'I suppose you're out after more animals. I can give you some advice. I can tell you where you can find rabbits and woodchucks, and porcupines and skunks.'

'Thank you so much,' said Hal, 'but we would be

afraid to tackle such savage animals. Don't you know of anything that won't bite?'

'Well,' said the proprietor, 'there's the lizard and the toad and the frog.'

Hal said, 'You're giving us some very valuable information. We'll look for some lizards and toads and frogs. You're quite sure that they don't bite?'

'I've never laid hands on them myself. That's the best policy. Leave them alone — then they can't hurt you.'

The landlord never suspected that Hal had been kidding him. Roger laughed when he heard about it. 'Well,' he said, 'we'd better get after those toads and frogs.'

The flight over hundreds of snowy peaks stabbing the sky was as exciting as it had been before. Nanook enjoyed the ride. He was not at all nervous, because he was travelling with the two humans he loved. They would take care of him and he would take care of them.

As soon as they had dodged one peak they faced another. It kept them a little breathless, not knowing at what moment they might collide with one of these towers of solid rock. Ben usually flew over them. But that was not so easy when he was toting half a ton of polar bear.

Smoke ahead told them that they were approaching the Valley of Ten Thousand Smokes. Martin Volcano was sending its white cloud of steam thousands of feet into the air. They passed over the great Katmai Volcano. A terrific eruption in 1812, which had spread a haze over half of the world's surface, was credited to Mount Katmai. The effects were felt in Europe, North America, Asia and North Africa. Volcanic ash a foot deep was laid down on Kodiak Island a hundred miles away. Violent earthquakes laid open the land and from the cracks there was a gigantic flow of red hot sand, which kept rolling fifteen miles, consuming everything in its path. Steam, boiling hot, spouted from the cracks, scorching anyone who happened to come near. That was the birth of the Valley of Ten Thousand Smokes.

Below them the crater of Katmai Volcano was eight miles wide. At its bottom they expected to see fire — instead there was a large lake.

The Valley of Ten Thousand Smokes had lost many of its smokes, but at least a thousand remained. The plane came down in the Valley, singeing the wings as they passed over a column of fire. If that fire had reached the tanks of gasoline there would have been an explosion that would end for good and all the Hunt expedition.

After visiting the fumaroles, as these jets of fiery steam were called, they flew back a few miles to Grosvenor Camp, named after the president of the National Geographic Society, which had originally explored this region.

Beside the camp was Lake Grosvenor and around it on all sides rose great volcanic mountains, Kaguyak still on fire, Griggs, Mageik, Martin blazing furiously, and many others, all well over a mile high.

The manager of Grosvenor Camp heartily welcomed the boys and their bear. Hal spoke to him about the great eruption.

'I was here when it happened,' said the manager. 'Of course I was a young man then. It scared me

198

half to death. The days were as dark as the nights. The earth kept shaking and fire spouted from the volcanoes. Hot ash covered the houses several feet deep. But not one person died. Vesuvius buried a whole city. That didn't happen here because there was no city.'

The boys spent a day exploring the Valley. Even where steam was not spouting up, the ground was so hot that they could not sit on it. Every once in a while there was a rumble beneath that shook the earth. There were deep gullies that had to be crossed. To go down fifty feet and climb up on the other side was exhausting. With every step their ankles sank into hot sand. At any moment their feet might start a burning avalanche that would carry them down with it. Nanook had less trouble. His clawed feet went down through the sand and clutched the rocks beneath. He climbed up the sliding slopes with ease. The boys found that the best way to get up was to hang on to Nanook.

Walking over the flat places, they found the earth so hot it nearly burned through the soles of their caribou boots.

They had brought along a can of food, but the food was cold. They attached a string to the can and let it down into a fumarole. After a few minutes it came up boiling hot. How convenient to have a stove waiting for you wherever you walked.

And if they wanted a cold drink, they had only to place their bottle, which had been warmed by the sun, upon one of the glaciers which came down from the mountains. In a few moments the drink was as cold as if it had contained ice cubes.

But this fascinating experience was not getting them an elk. The next morning they set out on a walk past Mount LaGorce to Hallo Bay. There they boarded a ferry which took them across Shelikof Strait to Afognak Island.

There was a dense fog. Roger said, 'The island has a good name — Afog. Is it always foggy here?'

Hal said, 'There's a lot of fog along this coast.'

They could see no elk. But suddenly they heard them. The orchestra of the elks — bugles, trumpets, trombones, saxophones, and the deep thunder of the tuba.

Hal remembered what Theodore Roosevelt had said: 'Heard at a little distance, it is one of the grandest and most beautiful sounds in nature.'

He was right. The song of the elks was a sound never to be forgotten.

Hal said, 'Any zoo would be tickled to death to get an elk just for its music alone.'

'Why did we have to come way down here to find elk?' Roger asked.

'There used to be plenty of them in Alaska, but the Indians killed them to get their two upper teeth.'

'Why in the world did they want them?'

'They used the teeth as ornaments to adorn their clothes. These were supposed to be charms to keep off evil. One Indian chief thought himself well protected because he had fifty elk teeth sewn to his garments. Thousands of elk were killed just for their teeth, and their bodies were left to rot. This island was off by itself and hard to get to so the elk that were here thrived and multiplied.'

Roger said, 'Since there are so few still alive I hate to take one of them.'

'But taking them is exactly what will keep them alive,' said Hal. 'Safe in a zoo, away from the charm hunters, they can raise their babies in peace, they can have medical treatment when they need it, and they will no longer be an endangered species. I mean they won't die out like so many other fine animals that have disappeared from the earth.'

Roger said, 'I heard the pilot say these were Roosevelt elk. Why are they called that?'

'Because Teddy Roosevelt took a great interest in them and in their fine music. These are the largest of all the world's elks. In honour of a great president they were named Roosevelt elk.'

The fog lifted a little and they could see the orchestra. It was a magnificent sight. More than a hundred of the great animals stood with their heads thrown back, pouring their music into the sky. Their splendid antlers almost touched their backs.

201

A man appeared. He strode up to the two boys and demanded, 'What do you want?'

'Is that any business of yours?' said Hal.

'It certainly is my business. I'm here to guard these animals. We have no use for charm hunters.'

'You're making a mistake,' said Hal. 'We are not charm hunters. We don't believe in charms to keep away the evil eye.'

'That's just so much talk,' said the guard. 'We've had a lot like you. You just want to murder an elk and cut out pieces of his hide and get his upper teeth and sell them to the Indians. I know your kind. Get off this island. There'll be no killing here.'

'Just what can we use to kill an elk? You can see that we have no rifles. I have a pocket knife — that's all. My brother doesn't even have that. I think he does have a toothpick. Do you think we could kill an elk with a toothpick?'

'Then why did you come here?'

'To hear the music. Also, we want to take one animal alive for a zoo. Our name is Hunt. Do you read the papers?'

'Of course I read the papers. Do you think I'm a dummy? Guess I owe you an apology.' He smiled for the first time. 'So you are the young fellows we've been reading about? Still I don't see how you are going to capture an elk with nothing but a toothpick.'

'How many elk do you have on the island?'

'Only three hundred. Every day we lose a few.'

'What do you mean — how do you lose them?'

'To charm hunters. And to these devilish wolves and wolverines and bears. They'd be much safer in a zoo. If you want one, take it — but I don't know how you're going to do it.'

'We'll find a way,' said Hal.

'Well, I must be getting on,' said the guard. 'Good luck to you.'

The boys, now on their own, puzzled over the problem of what to do. Hal had a lasso, but a powerful elk would snap it as if it were a thread.

'How about the sleep gun?' said Roger.

'The sleep gun would put an animal to sleep. Then how the dickens could we get him to the dock and on a boat? He'd just lie there until he woke up and we'd be no better off. We couldn't carry him. One of these big bulls must weigh at least eight hundred pounds and he's nine feet long.'

'If we had a helicopter,' Roger said, 'it would pick him up and carry him across the water to the Valley of Ten Thousand Smokes.'

Hal felt in his pockets. 'I have a handkerchief, and I have a little money, but, darn it, I don't seem to have a helicopter.'

Then the answer to their problem appeared. It was a ball of black fur from which stared two blazing red eyes.

'A wolverine!' exclaimed Hal.

It leaped up on the back of a great stag and sank its claws into the animal's flanks. A bad smell came from the shaggy little beast. It was a powerful musky odour. Roger held his nose.

'That's why they call it a "skunk bear",' said Hal.

The skunk bear fixed his large red eyes upon the boys as if daring them to do anything they could.

'He'll kill the elk,' said Hal. 'The wolverine kills just for the fun of it.'

The wolverine growled at the two humans and his growl developed into a roar that was louder than a bear's. He was small, not more than three feet long, but his terrible strength and fierceness were known throughout Alaska. The boys felt very helpless as they watched this furious beast.

But how about the lasso? It couldn't be used on the elk but it might do nicely in the case of the skunk bear.

Hal threw it over the wolverine's neck. Both boys

pulled with all the strength that was in them. The wolverine dug its claws more deeply into the suffering elk. The great bugler was not bugling now. He tried to scrape his enemy from his back with his horns but the wolverine had evidently taken that into account. He had positioned himself far enough back so that the horns did not reach him. When the elk grew weak with pain, his attacker would come forward and, clasping his sharp claws around the animal's neck, would choke him to death.

But this thing around his own neck — he didn't like it and tried to scrape it off. The boys could not pull him loose. Another bull came up. Roger had an inspiration. He made a loop in the other end of the rope and dropped it over the horns of the elk who had just arrived. Then he gave the animal a strong slap on the flank and the bull leaped away jerking the wolverine from the other bull's back. Hal flipped the lasso free.

The tortured elk was bleeding from the gashes made in his hide by the savage claws of the wolverine. Hal went into his pockets and found more than money and a handkerchief. He took out a tube of antiseptic salve and doctored the wounds of the injured elk. The intelligent animal stood still. He knew who his friends were. Besides, he was too weak to do any galloping.

'Let's start toward the dock and see if he follows,' said Hal.

The elk did follow, very slowly. He was trembling with pain. He kept looking from right to left, watching for other beasts that might do him harm.

205

With these two humans who had saved his life, he would be safe.

With them he went out on the dock and followed them as they boarded the ferry for the Valley of Ten Thousand Smokes. The manager of Grosvenor Camp, being an animal lover, warmly received this four-legged guest and gave him a stall in the barn with plenty of fodder of the sort that he liked best. As soon as a cargo plane was available he would be shipped south.

In the meantime he began to bugle, weakly at first, but soon he was trumpeting what Roosevelt had called, 'one of the grandest and most beautiful sounds in nature'.

32
The Horrible Grizzly

'In Latin it is called *Ursus horribilis*,' Hal said. '*Ursus* means bear and *horribilis*, of course, means horrible. And we have to get one.'

They were hunting by helicopter. Ben Bolt had consented to fly the boys and their Nanook to Kodiak Island and stay with them until they captured a grizzly.

'It sure is a new way to hunt,' said Ben. 'But it has its good points. It might take you weeks if you walked. Flying, we may come on one in a day or so. They say Grayback Mountain is the best place to find them. We'll just fly round and round Grayback, up and down, until we spot one. Then we'll land and grab him.'

It was not going to be quite that easy. They circled the mountain all day and saw nothing. At dusk they landed on the summit and put up their tent.

'Better luck tomorrow,' said Ben.

They had their 'better luck' sooner than that. A little past midnight Roger heard a snorting and snuffling just outside the tent. He nudged Hal. 'Wake up! There's your grizzly.'

Hal leaped up, grabbed his trousers, and was in

such a hurry that he put both his legs into the same leg. He hopped out of the tent and fell over the grizzly who was so astonished that he ran away as fast as his legs could carry him.

Ben woke up. 'What's going on?' he asked.

'Nothing much,' said Hal. 'Just taking a little exercise.'

'At midnight?' Ben turned on his torch. 'My word! A bear got one of your legs.'

Roger began to laugh and Hal joined in as he pulled his legs free and got back into his sleeping bag. Ben, going to sleep again, dreamed that his friend Hal was going about on crutches with one leg missing.

At breakfast, Hal had nothing to say about his somersault over the *Ursus horribilis*.

Ben talked about grizzlies.

'If you come anywhere near one, he'll kill you. Grizzlies have terrible tempers. There's only one bear more fierce, and that's the Kodiak bear. Your father wanted a white grizzly. There are very few of them left but some may be found here. The grizzly is hump-backed. He has a pushed-in face. Alaska has perhaps ten thousand grizzlies left but few of them are white. The cubs are very much like boys. They do not reach a good size until they are ten years old. A male grizzly can weigh as much as eight hundred pounds. A lot more than the black bear, which weighs about four hundred. Of course your dad doesn't want a black bear because there are plenty of them down south. A black bear can do something that a grizzly can't do. He can climb a tree. The grizzly is too heavy to do anything like that.'

'What does a grizzly eat?' asked Roger.

'He eats you, if he can get you. If he can't, he dines on chipmunks, mice, marmots, gophers and ground squirrels.'

'Can he run fast?'

'Twenty-five miles an hour. Then he gets tired.'

They spent the morning flying about Grayback. They saw squirrels and woodchucks, but no grizzly. It was almost noon before they spotted a big white rock. At least it looked like a rock. Ben was suspicious. He brought the helicopter to a halt fifty feet above the 'rock'. The rock got up on all four feet and turned his pushed-in face up so that he could look at this strange bird above him.

'That's our boy,' said Ben. 'His face is ugly but his snow-white body is a beautiful thing to see.'

'But how are we going to get him?' Roger asked.

'I'll let down a net,' said Ben. 'It will lie flat on the ground. Perhaps he will walk into it. Then we'll pull him up.'

'How can you pull up eight hundred pounds?' asked Hal.

'Not by hand,' said Ben. 'By machine. We have a hoist.'

The grizzly showed no desire to walk into the net. They waited patiently for a long time but it was no use.

'Someone will have to go down and attract him into the net,' said Ben. 'I have to stick by the helicopter. It's up to one of you two.'

Roger spoke up before Hal could. It would be an adventure, and Roger thirsted for adventure.

'I'll go down the rope,' he said.

'Wait a minute,' said Ben. He moved the helicopter twenty or thirty feet away so that Roger would not descend directly upon the bear.

Roger went down the rope hand over hand. As he reached the ground the grizzly welcomed him with a savage growl. Roger placed himself so that the net would be between him and the bear. He still hung on to the rope so he could climb it at any moment.

The grizzly moved toward him, growling softly. He was hungry, and here was his dinner waiting for him. Now the grizzly was in the middle of the net.

Roger, who had had plenty of experience in climbing a rope, went up about fifteen feet. 'All right,' he yelled, 'haul away.' Then the net tightened around the bear and he began to go up toward the helicopter.

Roger got there first. Ben shut off the hoist. He had no intention of sharing the cockpit with the horrible grizzly.

He changed the pitch of the rotor and the helicopter approached the airport. The net in which the bear was cradled swung about twenty feet below the aircraft.

Arriving over the airfield, Ben looked for a cargo van with an open hatch on top. When he found one he stopped the helicopter in mid-air directly above the hatch and let the net with the bear in it down into the van. The bear scrambled out of the net and the net was drawn up into the helicopter.

Mission accomplished.

The aircraft came to earth and Hal went to the office to arrange shipment of the van, locked upon the flatbed of a cargo plane, across Canada and the United States to a certain farm, where the *Ursus horribilis* would receive a hearty welcome from John Hunt.

33
Biggest Bear on Earth

'Now we just have to get a Kodiak bear and we're finished,' Hal said. He was talking to a captain at the Kodiak Naval Station.

The captain replied, 'You'll be finished all right if you tackle a Kodiak bear. He's a quiet fellow if you leave him alone. But if you interfere with him, you'll be sorry. Or, rather, you won't. You'll be too dead to be sorry.'

'I'm afraid we have no choice,' said Hal. 'Our father is a collector of wild animals for zoos. He has asked us to get a Kodiak bear. We've never failed to get him what he asked for.'

'Yes, but you've never tried to take the biggest bear in the world.'

'Really the biggest?'

'Really. Let me tell you about Alaskan bears. The male blue bear weighs 200 pounds. The black bear, 400. The grizzly, 800. The polar bear, 1,000. The Kodiak bear, 2,000. That's an average figure. Some weigh 1,500, some weigh 3,000. But the average is 2,000 pounds — twice the weight of any other bear on earth. He's not only the biggest in the world, he's almighty strong.'

'But you say he's quiet.'

'When he's let be. But there's one on that hill just behind the Naval Station that is mad enough to chew your head off.'

'Why?'

'A hunter shot his mate. Then somebody stole his two cubs. The big fellow went berserk. He's ready to eat anyone who comes near him. He was very fond of his mate and his young ones. Now he's just a big ball of wild, slashing fury. He's killing every person he can get his teeth into.'

A young fellow not in uniform, who had been listening, broke in with, 'Oh boy! What he needs is a bullet from this new gun of mine. Can I go with you?'

'No thanks,' Hal said.

'But you can't stop me.'

'No, I can't stop you. But if you get killed don't expect me to bury you.'

At the foot of the mountain the road split into two branches. Which should they take? Hal rapped at the door of a farmhouse. The door was opened by a surly fellow who said sharply:

'What do you want?'

'Which road do we take to get to the top of the mountain?'

'The one on the left,' snapped the farmer. 'But don't go up there.'

Hal said, 'We know about the bear who has lost his mate and his cubs. Has he done any damage here?'

'Killed twenty of my cattle,' said the farmer roughly.

'Have you any idea who stole his cubs?'

The farmer's face flushed. 'How the devil would I know anything about that? I live here alone. I don't get any news and that's the way I like it. I can't stand here wasting time on three kids. I told you which road to take. Now, get along. I'm busy.'

Just before the door slammed shut, the boys heard a small sound from inside.

As they started up the left branch, Roger said:

'Did you hear that? He said he lives alone. Then what could have made that sound?'

'A cat perhaps,' said Hal.

But he wondered.

The boys followed the dirt road up Sharatin Mountain. That was the name given to it on the map. The captain had called it a hill. Well, perhaps it was more than a hill and not quite a mountain since its height was less than three thousand feet.

The boy with the gun followed. His name, he said, was Mark.

Hal kept hoping that Mark would tire himself out climbing the steep slope — then he would turn about and go home.

'I'll protect you if you get into trouble,' said Mark.

'Your protection is the last thing we want,' Hal said. 'If you use that gun, I'll kick you all the way down hill.'

'But what's the use of having a gun if I don't use it?'

'Go shoot a hedgehog — or a gopher,' Hal suggested. 'But if you value your life, leave the bear alone.'

'Look!' exclaimed Roger. 'Right here beside the road.'

He picked up a jawbone. 'Some animal was killed here.'

Hal looked closely at the jawbone. 'That didn't come from any animal,' he said. 'That's human.'

Near by was a skull, and it certainly was the skull of a man. They found the dead body. On his wrist was a watch.

Mark removed it. 'I'll take that,' he said. 'Finders keepers.'

'Wrong,' said Hal. 'If you find something that belongs to someone else, you have no right to keep it.'

'But he won't have any more use for it.'

'His folks will probably come to find him. Anything on him belongs to them.'

Grumbling, Mark replaced the watch on the dead man's wrist. The body was spattered with dried blood. In the blood Hal saw brown hairs.

'Now we know what happened,' said Hal. 'This man was killed by that bear made crazy by the loss of his mate and cubs.'

'How do you figure that out?' Roger asked.

'These hairs came from a brown bear. That's the Kodiak bear. And the ordinary Kodiak bear is too quiet to attack a man unless he had good reason. This is the work of the bear we are after.'

A little farther on a whole tree had been torn up by the roots and lay on the ground, its leaves still green. Again there were brown hairs that told the story. Then they saw the remains of a black bear. It had been partly eaten. More brown hairs.

A small house had been completely wrecked. Some terribly powerful force had broken the walls and the roof had collapsed. A woman stood by the ruined house, weeping.

'He was always a good bear,' the woman said. 'Never hurt man, woman or child. But now something has got into him. He's gone plumb crazy.'

They came to a tent. The tent had not been attacked. But when they looked inside, they saw a man lying on the ground. Hal felt his pulse. He was dead.

They came to an empty cabin. Nobody would use it again for a long time. The windows were smashed, the roof torn off, the bunk destroyed, the sheet-iron stove had been flattened and the floor was covered with beans, rice, flour and coffee.

Reaching the top of the mountain, they found the great bear. He was sleeping, his head on the dead body of his mate. It is said that animals do not love. This scene impressed them all, for this showed the deep affection one beast may have for another. Hal and Roger were too old to cry, but tears came to their eyes.

Mark felt differently. He was going to kill this monster. He put his foot on the bear and fired. The bullet went through his foot. Mark howled to high heaven.

The bear did not stir. The bullet had not penetrated his heavy hide. He was so completely lost in misery over the death of his mate that he paid no attention to the boys. He would take care of them later.

Hal felt inclined to give Mark a good beating.

Instead, he looked at the injured foot. Luckily, no bones were broken since the bullet had simply gone through the fleshy part of the foot. After all, the bullet had been very small, coming from a low calibre .22 gun.

'Quit howling like a stuck pig,' Hal said to Mark. 'You're not badly hurt.'

The boys set up their own tent. It was nearly dark now and they hoped that the bear would stay exactly where he was until dawn. Mark crowded into the tent with them. He had no sleeping bag, but the night was not cold.

In the middle of the night Mark heard a rustling outside the tent. It must be the bear. He reached for his trusty pea-shooter, and prepared to be a hero. He was going to save the boys from certain death.

He separated the flaps just enough to get the muzzle of the gun out and he fired. He could see nothing, and he was not to know until morning that he had shot not the bear, but a mountain goat.

Aroused by the report, Hal said, 'You fire one more shot and I'm going to take that gun away from you.'

Mark fired one more shot. Dawn had come and he ventured out, holding his precious rifle. This time he saw the great bear itself, and there was no mistake. What a great story for the folks back home if he could just kill this monster!

He fired. The small bullet did not penetrate the tremendous hide of the bear. The Kodiak's skin has an elastic quality and the bullet ricocheted, bounced back, and struck Mark on the jaw.

Hal leaped up, seized the little rifle, and broke it over his knee.

Mark was whining about his dislocated jaw, not to mention his punctured foot.

There was a small village of not more than a hundred people on top of the mountain. After breakfast, Hal went to the village to find help for the banged-up youngster. He entered the tiny one-room post office. The staff consisted of one man only, the old post-master.

'We've had an accident,' Hal said. 'Is there a doctor in town?'

'No doctor. The nearest doctor is the surgeon down at the Naval Station.'

Hal said, 'A young fool of a boy has busted himself up. He needs a doctor.'

'I'll take him down,' said the postmaster. 'I have to go down anyway to get the mail.'

'Thanks a lot,' said Hal. 'That's mighty good of you.'

He sat down and wrote a note. It was addressed to Captain Sam Harkness and it read, 'Sending you a boy who has shot himself twice while trying to kill the Kodiak bear. Have Navy Surgeon fix him up and send him home before he makes a bigger fool of himself. I will pay any charges.' And he signed it, 'Hal Hunt.'

So Mark was transported to the Naval Station and Hal fervently hoped that he would never see him again.

Hal went to the police station. The little village had only one policeman.

'Would you go down the hill with us,' Hal said, 'to the farmhouse where the road divides?'

'That's Spike Burn's place,' said the policeman. 'He's a rough customer. What do you want to see him for?'

'This Kodiak bear that has gone crazy because he lost his mate and his cubs — there's nothing we can do about the mate. She's dead as a door nail. But if we could give him back the cubs, perhaps he would quiet down.'

'What has that to do with Spike?' asked the policeman.

'Perhaps nothing. Perhaps a good deal. When we talked with him we heard a sound inside that might have been made by a cat, or a bird — or by those cubs.'

'You think he was the one who stole the cubs?'

'It's just a guess. I can't barge into his house and make a search. But you can because you're a cop.'

'O.K.,' said the policeman. 'Here we go.'

Roger joined them and they went down the road to the farmhouse. The policeman carried a search warrant. They rapped, and Spike came to the door. He was highly displeased to see the policeman. 'What's up?' he said.

'May we come in and look around?' said the cop.

'You may not. You have no authority to do anything like that.'

'Here's the authority,' said the policeman, and he handed Spike the search warrant.

Reluctantly Spike let them in. They searched the house quite thoroughly and found nothing.

Then there was that sound again. 'What was that?' said the policeman.

'Just one of the doors. It creaks,' said Spike.

'Perhaps it's this door,' said the policeman, and he opened the door of a closet. And there they were, the two cubs.

'You'll get a heavy fine for this,' said the policeman. 'Why in the world did you steal these cubs?'

'Well,' said Spike, 'I was just going to fatten them up and then kill and eat them. A man must live, you know. Besides, the bear killed twenty of my cattle.'

The policeman said, 'You'll live long enough to pay handsomely for what you've done. Pick 'em up, boys.'

Hal took up one squirming little fellow in his arms, and Roger took the other. They climbed the hill and found the bear occupied in tearing down their tent. The great bear growled when he saw them coming. He was ready now to add them to his list of victims.

But when he saw the cubs his manner changed. They were set down gently in front of him. He licked both of them from stem to stern. He looked up at the boys and his eyes said, 'Thank you.' Most male bears pay no attention to their cubs. They leave that to the mother. But here there was no mother. And the great Kodiak was not only larger and stronger than others, but also more intelligent. When he lost his mate, he poured out his love on these little brats.

There was one telephone in town and that was in the postmaster's shack.

Hal telephoned to Captain Harkness. 'We've got the big bear,' he said. 'He's torn things up pretty badly, but he has his cubs now. You wouldn't believe

what a difference that has made. The happiest and sweetest old bear you ever saw.'

'How are you going to transport him?' the captain asked. 'Can we help? There's no war on at the moment and we have a lot of planes standing idle. You can use one if you wish.'

'That's just fine,' said Hal. 'The only thing is, how do we get the bear and his cubs down to you?'

'No need to do that. We'll send a transport plane up there. Is there any sort of a runway?'

'Not a real runway, but there's a long straight stretch that might serve.'

'I'll have a transport up there in half an hour.'

They did better than that. In twenty minutes a transport plane settled down on top of Mount Sharatin. The Navy had all sorts of planes, and the 'transport plane' was a boxlike affair quite strong enough to carry a 2,000-pound bear and his cubs, plus two boys whose work was done. The pilot was a brisk young fellow who had never seen New York and was delighted to have this chance.

'But how are you going to get the three bears into the plane?' he wanted to know.

'Very simple,' said Hal.

He picked up the two cubs and put them aboard. The big bear promptly followed them. The sliding door at the rear was let down.

'Got room for us too?' asked Hal.

'Sure. Right up in front with me,' said the pilot.

The great box, ten feet wide and as high as a room, trundled bumpily over the ground to the edge of a cliff and then launched out into space. At first it fell dizzily. But soon it was under control and

222

came down at the airport to pick up Nanook. This done, it rose into the sky, passed over the harbour and above the reef called Albatross Bank, where dozens of the great birds were fishing for salmon. Then in an almost direct line it flew over Juneau, Edmonton, Winnipeg and Toronto, over the skyscrapers of New York to come down at last on the Hunt Wild Animal Farm.

John Hunt looked with amazement at the great Kodiak bear.

'I always knew', he said, 'that the Kodiak was huge. But he's bigger than I ever imagined. A number of zoos have asked for him. I'm not going to give him to the zoo that offers the most money, but to the zoo that can care for him best and bring up those cubs to be as great as he is.'

He looked at his sons with great pride.

'You fellows deserve the best. These three bears will bring at least fifty thousand dollars. You've both told me you want to be naturalists. All right — that money will go into a trust for you so you can get the education you need to be wildlife scientists. You already know the outside of your animals. The time will come when you will know them inside out.'

ADVENTURE

The Adventure Series by Willard Price

Read these exciting stories about Hal and Roger Hunt and their search for wild animals. Out now in paperback from Red Fox at £3.99

Amazon Adventure
Hal and Roger find themselves abandoned and alone in the Amazon Jungle when a mission to explore unchartered territory of the Pastaza River goes off course...
0 09 918221 1

Underwater Adventure
The intrepid Hunts have joined forces with the Oceanographic Institute to study sea life, collect specimens and follow a sunken treasure ship trail...
0 09 918231 9

Arctic Adventure
Olrik the eskimo and his bear, Nanook, join Hal and Roger on their trek towards the polar ice cap. And with Zeb the hunter hot on their trail the temperature soon turns from cold to murderously chilling...
0 09 918321 8

Elephant Adventure
Danger levels soar with the temperature for Hal and Roger as they embark upon a journey to the equator, charged with the task of finding an extremely rare white elephant...
0 09 918331 5

Volcano Adventure
A scientific study of the volcanoes of the Pacific with world famous volcanologist, Dr Dan Adams, erupts into an adventure of a lifetime for Hal and Roger....
0 09 918241 6

South Sea Adventure
Hal and Roger can't resist the offer of a trip to the South Seas in search of a creature known as the Nightmare of the Pacific...
0 09 918251 3

Safari Adventure
Tsavo national park has become a death trap. Can Hal and Roger succeed in their mission of liberating it from the clutches of a Blackbeard's deadly gang of poachers?...
0 09 918341 2

African Adventure
On safari in African big-game country, Hal and Roger coolly tackle their brief to round up a mysterious man-eating beast. Meanwhile, a merciless band of killers follow in their wake...
0 09 918371 4

It's wild! It's dangerous! And it's out there!